autumn falls

autumn falls

a novel

BELLA THORNE

with **ELISE ALLEN**

DELACORTE PRESS

Text copyright © 2014 by Bella Thorne
Jacket photograph © 2014 by anneleven/Getty Images

randomhouseteens.com

Educators and librarians, for a variety of teaching tools, visit us at RHTeachersLibrarians.com

Library of Congress Cataloging-in-Publication Data
Thorne, Bella.
Autumn Falls : a novel / by Bella Thorne ; with Elise Allen.
pages cm
Summary: "Following her adored father's death, a teenager named Autumn Falls is forced to relocate to a new school in Florida for sophomore year. And when Autumn receives an enchanted gift—a journal that literally brings Autumn's writing to life—anything could happen. Could the journal be imbued with her dad's spirit?"—Provided by publisher.
ISBN 978-0-385-74433-1 (hc) — ISBN 978-0-375-99161-5 (glb) — ISBN 978-0-385-38523-7 (ebook)
[1. Magic—Fiction. 2. Diaries—Fiction. 3. Fathers—Fiction. 4. High schools—Fiction. 5. Schools—Fiction.] I. Allen, Elise, author. II. Title.
PZ7.T3923Au 2014
[Fic]—dc23
2014009484

The text of this book is set in 12-point Chaparral Pro.
Book design by Heather Kelly

Printed in the United States of America
10 9 8 7 6 5 4 3 2 1
First Edition

In loving memory of my father, grandmother,
and grandfather, who I believe are watching over me,
protecting and loving me from afar.

This book is dedicated to all my bellarinas/-os,
who have become my greatest supporters.
I hope you enjoy this story . . .
it is for you.

prologue

The day it happened, Jenna warned me it would end in di-saster. "Seriously, Autumn," she said, sitting down at my kitchen island and helping herself to an apple. "I think this is going to be a tragedy."

"Gee, thanks for the vote of confidence," I said, reaching for the glass mixing bowls on the top cabinet shelf. "I appreciate it." But it wasn't like she was crazy for saying it. Because first of all, I didn't know how to cook. Second of all, I was attempting one of my grandmother Eddy's trickiest Cuban recipes, *boniatillo*. And finally, I needed the outcome to be absolutely perfect so my father would understand that I was sorry.

I hadn't seen him in a month. He had his own busi-ness, and he traveled a lot. The company had something to do with computers, and I was vague about it not because he hadn't explained it to me, but because the explana-tion involved him speaking in technobabble, which was a

1

language I didn't understand. Big picture, he made secure storage systems for companies with huge amounts of massively important data that couldn't be lost or stolen without the world pretty much coming to an end.

Usually when he was away we'd have great nightly conversations. But during this trip I'd spent our phone convos accusing him of ruining my life and not caring about anybody but himself. And he wasn't away for work; he was in Florida, where his mom had had a stroke. He'd flown there the minute we heard the news, and stayed with her in the hospital for a full week on deathwatch.

Eddy made it, but she couldn't live by herself anymore, so Dad put her in assisted living. That should have been the end of it. Instead, he and Mom had a family meeting and decided we'd move from our suburb outside Baltimore to Aventura to be closer to Eddy and keep an eye on her.

Let the record show that this meeting included neither Erick nor me, even though together we made up half the family.

I didn't want to move. I'd lived in Stillwater all my life. Everyone I'd ever known and every memory I'd ever made was here. Stillwater was where I'd gone to elementary and middle school. Where I spent weekends hanging out with my friends at their houses and ordering pizza and Snapchatting silly photos of each other. It was where my best friend, Jenna, was—the one person who had seen me make a fool of myself during volleyball in sixth-grade gym class and risked her own popularity to sit with me at the lunch table. And shared her bag of homemade chocolate chip cookies. If Eddy needed help, why couldn't *she* move near *us*?

Of course Dad had a list of reasons. Eddy couldn't handle the cold winters, she needed familiarity, the cost of living was cheaper in Aventura, my parents had always talked about moving south one day, blah blah blah. It all meant the same thing: ripping me away from everything I loved in the middle of sophomore year without giving me any say.

So every time Dad called and tried to get me excited about the beaches and the food and our beautiful new house with a pool, I'd scream, beg him to change his mind, or go silent so he would really know how heartbroken and betrayed I felt. "If you loved me," I'd told him for the zillionth time the day before, "you wouldn't do this to me."

"I do love you, Autumn," he'd said, "which is why I made a decision."

"We're not moving?" I asked hopefully.

"We're still moving, but I'm stepping down as CEO. I'll consult, but I hired somebody to oversee the day-to-day stuff, including most of the traveling."

"You mean you'll stay home with us?"

The words had sounded unreal coming from my mouth. My whole life I'd been dying for Dad to do just that. To be there to high-five me when I got an A on a quiz, or drive me and Jenna to Target. To laugh at one of my jokes, or make me and Erick his famous banana-nut pancakes. To participate in my life instead of just being a bystander.

"But you always said no one else could handle things as well as you."

"Maybe I'm not as indispensible as I like to think," he said wryly. "I love you guys. I want this move to be a new beginning for us."

And suddenly I'd regretted all the grief I'd been giving him. I wasn't happy, but I could at least stop torturing him like a brat. I wanted to welcome him home with a grand gesture to show him how sorry I was. Hence the *boniatillo*.

"Okay," I said, checking out my staged tableau in the kitchen. "Three hours before we have to leave to get Dad at the airport. I've got the sweet potatoes, sugar, lime, cinnamon, and eggs. What else?"

Jenna tucked a strand of her dark hair behind her ear and looked down at my grandmother Eddy's long-ago-scrawled recipe. "A bottle of Manz . . . I have no idea what this means."

"*Manzanilla*." I pronounced it with a perfect Spanish accent. "It's a kind of wine." I opened the pantry door and clanked through the zillion dust-covered bottles.

"Party?" Jenna asked, waggling her perfectly plucked eyebrows.

I rolled my eyes. Jenna would never in a million years taste a drop of alcohol. It has nothing to do with the fact that we're only fifteen. Jenna's a runner. It's her Thing.

4

That's why she never wears more makeup than a little eye-liner and lip gloss, why her dark hair's always in a ponytail, and why she owns twenty pairs of sneakers. Sorry, *running shoes*. She doesn't eat and drink, she fuels and hydrates. Tainting her body with alcohol would be as great a sin as spilling a tanker full of oil into the ocean.

Me? I don't drink because my dad would kill me.

"Got it." I'd had to crawl into the pantry to dig out the bottle, and by the time I backed out, Erick had come downstairs and was filming while Jenna made goofy faces for the camera.

"Perv, cut it out," I said, pushing past him.

"What? I'm filming Jenna."

"And if I watched that, you're telling me I'd see her face and not her boobs?"

Erick gaped at me. "Well—"

"Seriously?" Jenna grabbed the camera. "Deleted," she announced as she erased it, then turned to me and added, "That I won't miss."

She wouldn't, but Erick would. He's four years younger than me, and Jenna and I have been friends since sixth grade, so he's known her for years and had a crush on her just as long. It used to be cute. Then he turned hideously prepubescent and became obsessed with . . . ugh.

"You have to stop, Icks," Jenna said as she handed him his camera. "I'm like your sister."

"You're *nothing* like my sister," Erick gushed.

"Gross. Hormone Boy, camera over here." I waited until

he had the lens aimed at me. "You want to catch this, because I, Autumn Falls, am about to cook."

"You want to get the fire extinguisher or should I?" Jenna asked Erick, causing him to crack up a lot longer than was really necessary.

"Laugh all you want," I said, ignoring them. "This could be a life-changing moment for me. Cooking could be my Thing."

I desperately needed a Thing. I was the only one in my house without one. Oh, sure, I had my Kyler Leeds obsession, but Jenna and I had a clear rule: people cannot be Things. Even if they could, it would take an actual boyfriend to qualify, not a rock star with whom I'd been hopelessly in love for two years.

Jenna and my family, meanwhile, were chock-full of Things. Mom had Catches Falls, her rescue organization for homeless dogs; Erick was all about his cameras; Dad had computers. Even my grandmother had a Thing. She'd been a potter back in Cuba. She gave it up when Dad was a baby and the family emigrated to the U.S. but took it up again after my grandfather died a couple of years later. She apparently supported the family selling her clay pots, which I find shocking. She gave Erick and me pots every year when we visited her in Florida, and honestly, they didn't seem so great. Not like something you could support a family on.

I wiped my hands on my jeans. I was covered in sweet-potato spatter and coated in sweat, and I'd shaved off the bulk of my finger skin with the vegetable peeler.

Cooking was not my Thing.

"Is this stuff supposed to look like old Play-Doh?" Erick asked, poking at the contents of a bowl.

"The recipe says it's supposed to be a smooth puree," Jenna said, wrinkling her nose. She and Erick exchanged glances.

"Shut up!" I snapped. I was bent over a saucepan filled with sugar, water, lime, and cinnamon. "How long do I have to stir this?"

" 'Until the syrup reaches the soft-thread stage,' " Jenna read.

"It's supposed to turn into yarn?" Erick asked.

"Jenna, please remove Erick from the area before I kill him."

"You're the one who wanted me to film this for Dad," he complained.

Our lazy bassett hound, Schmidt, woke from a sound sleep and started barking, which meant Mom was home.

"Mmmm, what's that smell?" she asked, walking in and dropping her yoga mat next to Jenna's tote bag. Anytime Dad came back from a long trip, Mom got so excited that only insanely exhausting exercise could keep her calm enough to function. They'd been married twenty years and she was still so in love that she'd jump out of her skin for him. "Are you making the *boniatillo*?"

Erick snorted. "Sort of."

"Do you need help?" Mom asked.

"I've got it," I insisted, feeling annoyed.

She came over anyway. "It gets a little complicated." She looked over my shoulder into the saucepan, then scooped up some syrup and let it drip back in. "You went a little long with the heat, but it's okay. I'd pour in the batter and keep stirring until it gets smooth. It'll be fantastic."

She kissed the top of my head before heading upstairs. I did what she said, but it didn't get smooth at all. It was like stirring concrete.

"He's going to think I'm poisoning him," I said through gritted teeth.

"It'll be okay," Jenna said in that reassuring way she had that made me feel grateful to have her and overwhelmingly sad that soon I wouldn't.

"Hey, look at that!" Erick shouted. "It's smoothing out. You really did it, Autumn."

It didn't happen often, but sometimes Erick completely forgot to be a pain. He zoomed his camera in for beauty shots while Jenna read off more directions and I took the pot off the heat, waited a bit, then added two beaten egg yolks, stirred the whole thing over the burner some more, put in the Manzanilla, then poured it all into a soufflé dish.

"By the time Dad's here," I announced to the camera in my best celebrity-chef voice, "it'll be chilled and ready to enjoy with a dollop of fresh whipped cream."

Jenna applauded as I bowed.

"I'm gonna post this, okay?" Erick asked in a non-asking kind of way.

Erick had his own YouTube channel, but Dad had made him promise never to post footage of anyone without their permission.

"Bad idea," Jenna said.

I checked out the freeze-frame of me. Clumps of sweet-potato goo stuck to my face and clotted my long orange hair. Add in my vegetable-peeler-bloodied fingers and I looked like a farmland horror show.

"Nice try," I said. "Not a chance."

I looked at the clock. I'd need every second if I was going to look human before we left to pick up Dad. "Jenna—"

"Go get ready. Text me later and tell me how it went." She chucked her apple core in the trash and hugged me despite my potatoey grossness, which is the measure of a true friend. Erick was still staring after her out the living room window when I headed upstairs to shower.

"Erick. It's so not happening," I said, just loud enough for him to hear.

▼

An hour and a half later, Mom and I were ready. "Erick! Let's go!" Mom called impatiently. She looked really pretty—she was wearing a skirt and top Dad had gotten her last Christmas, and her hair was shiny and smelled like mangoes. I don't know how the hair genes missed me, but they totally did. Hers is long, dark, and naturally curly. I'd tortured mine with a hair dryer, a curling iron, and mass quantities of styling product, and it was still a sea of orange limptitude with a faint sweet-potato scent.

"Coming!"

Mom tapped her hands against her sides, eager to get on the road. When her phone rang, she rummaged through her bag to find it. Her brows furrowed. "Hello? Yes, this is she. . . . I'm sorry, what?"

I'd been petting Schmidt, but when she said that, I froze. There was just something about her voice. Her face was pale, and she held the back of one of the kitchen chairs so tightly her knuckles went white.

"Okay, I'm ready!" Erick ran downstairs, but I met his eyes and shook my head.

"That's not possible," Mom said thickly. Erick and I both moved closer to her, but she wasn't looking at either one of us. "My husband's on a plane. We're about to go pick him up."

My breath caught in my throat. Jenna's prediction came floating eerily back to me. Erick reached for my hand and I took it.

"Yes," Mom said, the word barely more than a whisper. "Yes . . . that's his ring. Yes, on his right ankle. I understand, I . . . Yes."

She staggered to a drawer and pulled out a pen and paper, scrawling something down.

"Of course," she whispered. "Thank you."

She hung up the phone and leaned heavily on the counter, facing away from us, her head bent low.

"Mom?" I said. I sounded like a frightened little girl. "Is Daddy . . . ?"

Mom turned around. Her face was red and splotchy. It took her a long time before she could get out the words.

"There was a car accident near the airport in Miami," she said, her voice hollow. "Daddy never made it to the plane."

1

six weeks later

"Are you *kidding* me?"

I say it out loud because it's inconceivable any place could be this hot and sticky before eight a.m. My pleated-waist shorts are wrinkling in weird places, and I'm re-thinking the muscle tee over tank top that looked cute in the mirror but now just looks meh. The air is so thick it feels like the inside of a sweaty sneaker.

At least I don't have to rush. Aventura High's only six blocks away. And I'm not exactly in a hurry to get there. It hasn't been a great morning. Erick was flying his remote-control helicopter pre-dawn, and the thing zoomed into my room, and just as I lifted my head to flip my pillow over, it smacked into me. Hard.

"Owwww!" I cried out as the helicopter bounced off my forehead and landed on my comforter, writhing and twist-ing. I was already feeling pretty down. I feel that way a lot,

13

lately. The worst times are those moments right between sleeping and waking up.

When I'm asleep, he's alive.

When I'm awake, I pretend he's alive. I fool myself into thinking he's not gone, he's traveling. Just like always.

But when I'm in that thick, swimmy place, my senses just waking to reality, it smacks into me, just like Erick's stupid helicopter did: He's gone. Forever. And all I see are the scary accident-scene images I force away every other minute of the day and night.

So not only was I miserable, I was in serious pain—the maximum-dose ibuprofen kind.

"Autumn!" Erick said in this accusing tone as he ran in and picked it up. "That was my sky cam. Thanks a lot."

"Sky cam?" I watched as he detached one of his small camcorders from the bottom of the helicopter. "Seriously? You were filming me sleep?"

"Mom told me to wake you up! You slept through your alarm." Then he picked up a sock I'd left on the floor and slam-dunked it into my hamper. "Suh-weet! Falls does it again!"

Not true. I didn't *set* my alarm.

I blinked hard to clear my throbbing head. My brother looked like a kid on a cereal commercial, all bright-eyed and carefree, ready to tackle the day with the help of a good, balanced breakfast. It kind of made me nauseous.

"How are you happy?" I blurted out.

"What?"

"Aren't you nervous about the first day of school?"

"No," he said.

"You should be," I told him, my eyes narrowing. "It's all new kids. What if nobody likes you?"

"People will like me." He said it with conviction, but there was doubt in his eyes. I felt a flicker of triumph.

"Maybe they won't." I fixed him with a cold stare. "It's the middle of the year. Everyone already has their friends. Maybe they'll think you're some strange intruder who does freaky things like record people in their sleep, and no one will want to hang out with you at all."

Erick's mouth dropped open and the confidence drained out of his eyes. It felt satisfying . . . until he turned around and left, his shoulders hunched.

Then I knew I was the most horrible human being in the universe.

Because what I told him was really how I'm feeling about myself. My brother will be fine. I'm the one no one will want to hang out with. The one who won't fit in.

"Erick, wait!" I called, guilt filling me. "You left your sky cam!"

"I don't want it."

"Erick!" I'd make it up to him later. It's not that I wanted to be mean to Erick; he's just handling everything so much better than I am.

I plucked my phone from my night table and texted Jenna two words: I SUCK. Then I dragged myself to the bathroom and looked in the mirror. I had a giant red lump in the center of my forehead. One of the sky cam's propellers had sliced a cleft right in the middle of the bump, so the end result looked almost exactly like a monkey's swollen butt.

After a shower that only made the lump even larger and more horrifying, I went back to my room to find my mom on my bed.

"I know," I said when I saw her reproachful look. "I'm a terrible sister."

She just patted my pillows, so I sat down next to her. I'm a little taller than she is, which is still kind of weird. Like I'm supposed to be the one taking care of her because I'm bigger.

She put her arm around me and I leaned my head down on hers. "Do I have to go to school?"

"Ever?"

"Is never an option?"

"Do you remember why Daddy named you Autumn?" she asked.

"Because he secretly hated me?"

Think about it—*Autumn Falls*. It's a full declarative sentence that calls me out as a complete klutz *and* seasonally challenged. Here's Autumn. What does she do? She falls. Then there's the other problem. Summer is hot and beachy and outdoorsy and alive; winter is cozy and snowy and tucked in and sleepy. Autumn goes back and forth, not sure what it wants to be. It's a messy season, scattered and uncertain. And *that's* the season I'm named after. Twice.

Is it any wonder I've never found my Thing? No, it is not.

"He named you twice for what he thought was the most outstanding season of the year," Mom said.

"That's what he thought?" I asked. I know the story, but I wanted to hear her tell it.

"I had a whole list of other girl names, but he only wanted Autumn. He said he'd spent a lot of time getting to know you, and you were definitely Autumn Falls."

"Getting to know me . . . before I was born."

"That's what he said. And he said you were meant to be Autumn because autumn is complex. It's hot and it's cold, it's a wild mix of colors, and even when its leaves dry out and wither, it's still beautiful. 'Autumn is strong and intricate,' he told me, 'and our daughter will be too.'"

"So you're saying I have to go to school?" I asked, sighing heavily.

"I'm saying you're tougher than you think. Whether you go to school or not is up to you. I've got to drive Erick now. I love you, Autumn."

I flopped back on my bed, fully intending to go back to sleep . . . only I couldn't close my eyes. Stupid story. I wanted to be strong for my dad. The bump was still a problem, but a little makeup and a strategic shifting of my bangs helped.

When I got downstairs, my mom and Erick were gone.

For a second I gazed at the couch, the dog, and the TV. The three of us could have had a spectacular day together.

Then I picked up a framed photo on the end table. It's my dad, from our vacation in Bermuda just last August. He's standing on the pink sand in a superhero pose, pulled up tall with his hands on his hips. He'd lost his sunglasses the day before, so he was wearing a pair of mine that were round and bedazzled, and board shorts covered with Tiki-faced caricatures of U.S. presidents.

He's unbelievably goofy, but he's happy. You can tell. You hold the picture and it's like you can't help but want to jump in and hang out with him because you know you'll have the best time ever.

"I love you, Daddy," I said.

Then I walked out the door.

▼

As I pass a steady stream of single-story houses with pink roofs and huge picture windows, Jenna finally texts me back:

There is no U in Suck!

I miss her like crazy.

I still can't believe I'm living in Florida. I was positive that after what happened we'd cancel everything, but Mom decided Dad would want us to stick with our plans, move into the house he'd already set up for us, and keep an eye on Eddy. I argued that moving meant we'd lose our home and friends and everything familiar, which was one thing before, but now everything had changed. As a good mother, shouldn't Mom want us to hold on to what little stability we had left?

That made her cry. I've been a real rock for my family lately.

A block into the walk, a guy my age with a backpack slung over his shoulder turns onto the sidewalk from another street. I'm maybe four feet behind him, and I'm guessing he's also going to school because he looks the right age and has a backpack slung over one shoulder, and we make the exact same turns two blocks in a row.

I don't mean to stare at him, but he's right there in front of me, so I kind of do. He's wearing cargo shorts that reach to just above his knees, and a red T-shirt. I have an excellent view of the back of his head, which features close-cropped brown hair, but I'm particularly mesmerized by his neck. It's almost as red as his shirt. He must have forgotten to put sunblock there, because it's the only swath of burn I see, and this is a guy who'd burn easily. His arms and legs are as pale as mine, and I have to put on SPF 100+ if I even think about stepping outside around here.

Am I actually as pale as him? He's pretty translucent. I hold up my arm and try to judge it against his legs. It's a tough call with the distance between us. Maybe if I get a little closer.

I'm about to speed up when he wheels around.

"Either you're a private investigator on my tail, in which case I'll go ahead and tell you whatever you need to know, or you're also walking to Aventura High, in which case it's impossibly rude and maybe a little bit sexist to stay three steps ahead of you all the way to school."

I like him right away. Partly because he's funny and confident, partly because he's a fellow pale in a land of golden tans.

"I'm walking to Aventura High," I say. "Autumn Falls." He looks like he's thinking about it so I clarify. "My *name* is Autumn Falls. That's not just a statement I'm telling you."

"A Lustful Man," he says.

"Excuse me?"

"Anagram of your name. I'm J.J. Austin, which tragically has no good anagrams. One more 'A' and one more 'N' and I could be Just A Ninja, but as it is I've got nothing."

"This is what you do?" I ask as we start walking again. "You make anagrams?"

He nods. "I like word stuff. Anagrams, crosswords, acrostics, the jumble . . ."

"The *jumble*? Is that even a thing if you're under eighty?"

"It is if you're a member of my family. It's what we do together. Weird, I know, but it's kind of our thing."

"A full-family Thing?" I ask, impressed. "I didn't know that was possible."

I explain my theory and how the Family Thing will be a welcome addition to the treatise. I've spent all of five minutes with J.J. and I'm already acting like a goofball around him. I hope we have some classes together.

My new high school is a low, sprawling building in a truly bizarre shade of purple with AVENTURA HIGH painted in giant turquoise letters along the largest wall. It's shaped like a U, with a wide, flat lawn in the middle. The lawn is packed with people playing Frisbee, tossing footballs, and hanging out.

Maybe J.J.'s a good omen. Maybe I'll click this easily with everyone here. Maybe by next week—maybe by tomorrow morning—I'll have my own little spot on the lawn where my new amazing friends will meet me and hang out until class.

"Can you show me where the principal's office is?" I ask when we enter the building. Thankfully, it's air-conditioned, although it's too late now; I know without looking that my hair is a lost cause. "I'm supposed to check in with her."

"Sure. It's down this way. Did you just move here?"

I really preferred where the conversation was before. This road leads to my dad, which leads to wide, sympathetic eyes and a horrible you-poor-thing-I-can't-possibly-relate void that swallows everything it sees.

"Yeah. A couple weeks ago." I'm afraid he's going to start asking me questions, so I throw him off by asking for anagrams of Stillwater (Little Wars), Aventura (Rave Tuna), and Way Too Humid (Audio Myth Ow). By that time we're at the principal's office. It has a giant window that opens on the hall, but the blinds are shut tight.

"Want me to wait?" he asks. "I can walk you to your class."

"Oh," I say, not expecting that. "I'm good." I pull my tank top back and forth, trying to cool off.

"Got it."

I'd actually love it if he hung out and walked with me to class, but I don't want him to hear whatever the principal has to say. If she brings up my dad, it would just be awkward.

"So, I'll, um . . . see you around?" I offer.

"Right. See you around." He turns and walks away, then wheels back to call over his shoulder, "No Arduous Eye!" which I figure out is an anagram for "See you around."

As he walks off, I rummage in my tote bag for my phone and send Erick a text: sorry about this morning. the kids at school will love you.

He texts back immediately: I know they will. I'm awesome.

Sometimes I totally want to be my brother.

2

Mrs. Dorio barely glances up, just peers over her glasses when I walk into her office after the secretary motions me in. "Yes?"

"I'm Autumn Falls. I'm supposed to see you before I go to class?"

"Right." She rises and looks me over. Mrs. Dorio is young and could even be pretty if she weren't so intimidating. She doesn't crack a smile, possibly because she's roasting inside her gray pantsuit. "Did you get into a fight?"

Her words are clipped and almost monotone, as if she doesn't want to waste time or emotion on them. She walks around her desk so she can peer down at my forehead. Talking to J.J., I forgot all about the clefted lump of doom, but under her scrutiny it starts throbbing all over again.

"No. I, um—"

"Battery's an expellable offense. As are drugs, weapons on campus, sexual assault, and arson. Other offenses go through discipline council and result in anything from detention to expulsion depending on the severity and frequency of the crime. You received all this in our emails, yes?"

I have no idea what to say. Arson? Is that seriously a problem here?

Mrs. Dorio raises an eyebrow. I worry she's getting suspicious because I haven't responded. Maybe she thinks she struck a chord with the arson thing. "Yes," I say. "I got the emails."

"Good. Then you know where to go?"

"I do."

She stares at me again, waiting for more, so I pull out the schedule I printed.

"First period, room three. Ms. Sklowne."

Mrs. Dorio frowns and takes the paper.

"Ms. *Knowles*," she corrects me. "Room *eight*."

I would have gotten it right if she hadn't been looming over me. Still, she goes down the rows of classes and locations, pointing to the words as she reads them. It's mortifying, but I have to admit it helps. Now I won't have to worry about the letters and numbers playing tricks on me when I look at them later.

"Thanks."

She nods. "Welcome to Aventura High, Autumn. If you need anything, my door is always open."

As she says it, she pulls open her very *closed* door without a hint of irony, then shuts it again behind me.

The halls are empty. Class has already started. Great. I have my locker information, but there's no time to drop off my stuff; I'll just bring my whole bag. I walk as fast as I can, trying to strike a balance between speed and making sure my shoes don't echo too loudly on the linoleum floors. The walls are white, but with giant random swaths of turquoise and hot pink. I wonder if whoever painted the school was color-blind.

There's a window in the door of room 8, and I can see there's one open seat. It's across the room, but toward the back, so maybe I can slide in without the entire world coming to a screeching halt. It helps that I can hear the muffled voice of Ms. Knowles calling roll, so I know I'm not that late. It's possible they'll barely notice me.

When I open the door, a hundred pairs of eyes turn and stare.

Okay, maybe not a hundred. Maybe only twenty-five or so. It just *feels* like a hundred. I smile casually and walk toward the empty seat. I'm almost there when Ms. Knowles picks her head out of her attendance book. "Autumn Falls?"

I jerk my head up, which means I don't see the outstretched legs in front of me. Big surprise: I trip and sprawl to the ground and my bag spills open, stuff flying everywhere.

A few people laugh, including the guy with the hazardous legs. Then he gets inspired. "Check it out," he says. "*Autumn . . . Falls!*"

It's an oldie, but not to this crowd. Now they're all laughing. Even Ms. Knowles puts a hand over her mouth so I won't see her joining in.

I peek over my shoulder at the genius wit who made the comment. He's so enormous his desk/chair combo looks like a toy. I bet if he flexed, the whole setup would explode into shrapnel.

"You okay?"

I'm so busy looking at the Hulk I don't even notice the guy next to him slide out of his chair, but here he is next to me on the floor, and . . .

Oh.

He is easily the most beautiful human being I have ever seen in my life.

No, really. He could give Kyler Leeds a run for his money. Kind blue eyes, creamy dark skin, sculpted arms. He's picking up my pens and keys and lip gloss, and as he does, his flexed bicep curves out from his short-sleeved T-shirt. I wonder if he'd think it was weird if I traced it with my finger.

Oh no. I'm actually reaching out to trace it with my finger. Bad finger. I pull it back and hope he didn't notice.

"Don't you want them?" he asks.

His biceps? Yes, very much.

Then I realize he means my books. I take them and slide them back into my bag. "Thanks."

"No problem. I'm Sean."

"Autumn. Nice to meet you."

"Are you done making introductions on all fours like dogs," asks Ms. Knowles, "or do you still need to sniff each other's rear ends?"

More laughter. I quickly slip into my chair and slouch down. I feel bad for Sean. But he's laughing right along with everyone else. He even catches my eye and flashes a smile so bright I have to smile back.

As a rule I don't like to pigeonhole people, but Sean's pretty easy to peg: confident, gorgeous, fearless in the face of embarrassment . . . he's popular. Probably has been since birth. Good for him. And good for me. He was nice to the new girl; maybe that'll start a trend.

I feel a tap on my shoulder and turn to face a girl who's obviously just slumming here between takes for her swimsuit-issue cover shoot.

"Hi," she whispers, flashing a smile.

"Hi."

"I just wanted to let you know"—she leans over her desk and whispers a little louder—"you have a *growth* on the front of your head."

Everyone in earshot turns to stare, and it's like their eyes push down on the giant clefted lump, making it hurt worse than ever. I don't have to reach up to check. I know my bangs have shifted and it's out for all to see.

There's a terrible moment of silence; then a few people start to laugh.

And it's official: I've definitely been noticed. Just not in the way I hoped.

3

Stupid lump. Stupid sky cam. Stupid Erick.

I feel like walking right back out of this place, but it's not in my DNA to do something like that. I have Good Girl on autopilot. So I stay in school. I keep my head down and my mouth shut, and reach up every two seconds to tug on my bangs and make sure they cover my forehead deformity.

In other words, I look like a mental patient.

The one time I do open my mouth, it's to practice r trills in French, and I end up trilling a piece of gum out of my mouth and onto my neighbor's desk.

Lunch offers a welcome relief. At least I expect that to suck. After I finally drop my stuff in my locker, I walk through "the Tube," the long cafeteria building where everyone buys their food. I take my time snagging the least toxic-looking options. Eventually, though, I have to come out to the big grassy courtyard and the giant sea of strangers gathered in well-established groups at picnic tables or spots on the lawn.

Better to sit alone than stand around looking lost. I head for an empty spot on the grass, off to the side where I won't be noticed. It's Jenna's lunch period back in Stillwater too. Maybe she'll have her phone on.

"Autumn! *Autumn!*"

I wheel around and see J.J. waving to me, a big smile on his face.

He's with two other people: a scrawny, sandy-blond guy bent over his cell phone, and a short, curvy girl in a clingy tangerine-colored dress. She's sprawled sideways on the lawn, propped up on one elbow.

"Hey, J.J."

"Hey. Autumn, this is Jack Rivers and Amalita Leibowitz, alternatively known as Vicar's Jerk and Await A Zombie Lilt. In keeping with your theory, Amalita's Thing is cosmetics, while Jack's is comic books. In other words, Ames is dedicated to inspiring attraction between men and women, while Jack is dedicated to poisoning it."

"Dude, you're crazy," Jack retorts. "Girls love superheroes."

"Girls love guys who play superheroes in movies," Amalita counters, "not pasty boys who read about them."

"Watch with the pasty," J.J. says. "I prefer vampire chic."

Jack looks up at me for the first time. "Oh, hey—you spit gum on Carrie Amernick's desk in French class. Well done. She's evil."

"Not every girl who rejects you is evil," Amalita says. Then she turns to me and adds, "*Esta como una cabra* because she wouldn't go out with him but she went out with J.J.*"

"You speak Spanish?" I ask.

"Fine, so she's not evil," Jack says. "She just has crap taste."

"*Or* she likes talking about things other than villainous plans to take over Megalopolis," J.J. says.

"*Metropolis*, dude." Jack turns to me, but gestures to J.J. "He's a—"

"Yeah?" J.J. cuts him off. "Well, you're a—"

Amalita holds up a hand to ward them off and turns back to me. "*Sí. Y tu?*"

"*Solo un poco*," I say. "I'm half Cuban."

"Me too!" Amalita says. "I'm a PuertoMecuadorbano Jew. My mom's side is *Puerto* Rican, *Mex*ican, *E*cuador*ian, and *Cubano* . . . and my dad won't mix milk and meat."

"With me, it's my dad," I say. "He's—"

Was. He *was.* I blink back tears and hope they don't notice.

"Give me your face," Amalita says.

That's a bad idea. All she'll do is give me crap about my forehead and I swear I can't handle any more of it.

I also can't handle fighting back right this second, and there's no room in her eyes for a no. I lean forward, and Amalita's earrings and all her bracelets jangle as she sits up and takes my chin in her hands.

"Here's what I'd say," she offers after several long minutes. "You need to stay natural. Swap the lipstick for gloss. Peachy. Kill the eye shadow. Brown liner. Smudge it on top. On the bottom you need powder, the tiniest bit. Right now it's running down your face. Just a little, don't freak out, but it won't do that with the powder. Tiny bit of bronzer right here, on the apples of your cheeks. I see you wearing more, I smack you and take it away. We'll go to the mall after school and get everything you need, fifty dollars tops. Plus a little arnica gel. Put that on your head, ice it up tonight, the lump is gone by morning."

This time I don't even feel the tears coming. I just start to cry.

It's ridiculous. All she did was give me a beauty regimen. Now she probably thinks I'm crazy.

I clench my fists and take a deep shaky breath. Two more and I'm back to normal. I blot my eyes with a napkin and laugh it off. "Sorry," I say. "That was weird."

Amalita, J.J., and Jack exchange a look, no doubt silently figuring out how to slip away and enjoy the rest of their lunch period without the insane new girl. Then Amalita puts her hand on mine.

"We're sorry about your dad," she says softly.

Tears well up again and I have to swallow hard to stop them.

"How did you know?"

"I Googled you," Jack says sheepishly. "Beginning of lunch. J.J. wouldn't keep his mouth shut about you, so—"

He stops talking when J.J. punches his arm. J.J.'s face is the color of his sunburned neck. "There was an article in the paper about your mom's dog rescue," he explains. "It mentioned what happened. I'm really sorry."

I don't know if he means he's sorry about my dad or looking me up, but I guess it doesn't matter. I know the article Jack found. Mom had worked hard to set up the Aventura branch of Catches Falls before we even left Maryland, and she'd been happy to do an interview about it. She just didn't expect them to go with the tragic angle.

It actually feels good that someone here knows, but I can't say that out loud without crying again so I just nod.

"Oh, hell . . ."

J.J. says it under his breath and at first I think it's about me. Then I realize he's looking at Amalita, who's getting to her feet.

"Taylor!" she cries, waving her arm. "Tee! Hey, it's me! Don't you want to come hang out?"

"She's going to get us killed," Jack mutters.

I follow Amalita's gaze and my stomach turns. She's waving across the lawn to Miss Supermodel from first period. She walks in a pack with a tall blonde, the beast from class, and a couple of his equally beefy friends.

"What's the matter, Tee?" Amalita cries. "Did you lose your hearing and vision along with your memory? I'm right here!"

People everywhere are staring. The blonde looks furious. She and the supermodel have some kind of a conversation, but they're too far away to tell what it is. The guys stand around with their arms folded, like angry bodyguards. Then the blonde shakes her head and walks our way.

"At least she's alone," Jack says.

"Ames, let it go," J.J. advises. "No good will come of this."

If Amalita hears him, she doesn't show it. She waits for the girl with a huge smile on her face.

"What's going on?" I ask J.J.

"That's Taylor Danport," he says, nodding at the blonde. "She and Ames were best friends until exactly three months ago, when Taylor ditched her to start hanging out with Reenzie."

"Reenzie?"

"Marina Tresca. The brunette."

"She's evil," Jack says.

"For real this time," J.J. says. "It's true."

"What the hell are you doing?" Taylor hisses when she gets close to Amalita. "You're embarrassing yourself."

"I'm not embarrassed at all," Amalita says way too loudly. "Maybe you're the one who's embarrassed because you know what you did."

"Let it go," Taylor says, dropping her voice even lower.

"Let *what* go?" Amalita asks innocently. "The fact that you're a complete fake? That before this year your new *cuate* didn't even care that you were alive?"

"Hey there!" Reenzie chirps. I hadn't even noticed her

walking this way, but now she's at Taylor's side. She's a couple inches shorter than Taylor, but it's pretty obvious she's the one in charge. She smiles down at J.J. and Jack. "Guys, I don't know if you're aware, but there's still a ban on pit bulls in Miami-Dade County. I'd recommend you get yours to stop barking, or it'll have to be destroyed."

"Hi, Reenzie," Amalita says. "How was your break? Did you talk to Kaitlin? You know, the friend you ditched before you stole away Tee? Or how about Evelyn, the one before her? It's funny, you'd kind of have to be brain-dead to think you'd actually be loyal to anyone."

"Ames. Do you seriously think this makes me want to hang out with you again?" Taylor doesn't wait for an answer. She stalks off.

"Lighter fabrics," Reenzie says to Amalita. "They won't bunch and wrinkle so much in unsightly places." Then she turns to me. "Glad to see you've found your people. Pro tip," she adds, gesturing to my forehead, "you want to take care of that out here. Heat can make breakouts even worse."

As Reenzie joins Taylor, Amalita calls after them, "Hey, Tee! Don't forget I have pictures of you dressed as Super Grover! From *last year!*" She plops back on the grass and turns on the guys. "What is wrong with you? You didn't stick up for me. What are you, afraid of her?"

"You started it," Jack points out.

"And no, we're not afraid of Marina Tresca," J.J. adds. "But yes, if possible, we'd rather avoid her steroid mafia."

"Ignore them," Amalita tells me as I self-consciously touch my golf ball–sized lump. "Nothing she says matters."

But I can tell by her defiant yet sad expression that it does.

"Hey . . . did you mean it about hitting the mall after school?" I ask. "'Cause the stuff you were talking about . . . it sounds really good."

Amalita breaks out a smile. "Meet me at the front door right after eighth period," she says, her eyes smiling. "You will love what happens when you put yourself in my hands."

I kind of already do.

4

We're coming out of the cosmetics store when we see them. This is after Amalita and I spent two hours sampling products and comparing brands. Amalita clearly knows her stuff. She gave a running commentary on each one's quality, coverage, and staying power and explained which celebrities endorse the brand versus which ones actually use the product and look good. Kyler Leeds's stylist, apparently, is a big fan of Amalita's favorite hair-care line, and that little nugget of information leads us both into a major Kyler lovefest, during which we realize we'll doubtlessly have to wrestle to the death one day to decide which of us gets to be with him.

Reenzie, Taylor, and the big guy are coming down the escalator. They don't see us. Yet.

I grab Amalita's arm. "We should go back in the store. I think I do want to get that under-eye moisturizer after all."

"I'm not afraid of Reenzie," she says, staring at them. "You shouldn't be either."

"I'm not. It's just when I see a hornet's nest, I don't go out of my way to stomp on it."

"You sound like Jack and J.J." She gives me a stony-eyed look. "If you want to go stealth, you're hanging out with the wrong girl. I put it out there."

"I think that's great, I just—"

"Autumn!"

Amalita and I both look up. It's Sean. He must have been behind his giant friend. I haven't seen him since first period, and I thought maybe I'd overblown in my head how gorgeous he was.

I hadn't. And now he's walking right up to me.

"I thought maybe we'd have another class together, but I guess not," he says.

"No, guess not," I echo stupidly.

This is weird. Last time I saw him he was smack in the middle of a crowd of people laughing at me, but now he's saying he was looking for me in his classes?

I want to keep my bull detector on high alert, but it's hard when I can't think about anything beyond his eyes and his smile.

"Oh, did you guys officially meet?" he asks, as if just realizing he's with three other people. "Taylor, Reenzie, Zach . . . this is Autumn."

The three of them still hang back several feet. Zach

holds up a hand; Reenzie and Taylor give pained smiles, which I return. I don't even want to look and see what Amalita's doing next to me.

"Are you having dinner here?" Sean asks. "We were talking about heading to the food court. Maybe you could join us."

"That's a fantastic idea!" Amalita gushes. "Isn't that a fantastic idea, Tay? We could eat at Blackbeard's Burgers. Remember when you weren't all about what everyone else thought and we'd always put on the pirate hats? Here, I think I have pictures."

She pulls out her phone, and I'm convinced Taylor's going to swat it out of her hands. Before she can, Reenzie pipes up.

"Ooooh, wish we could." She sounds as sincere as a reality-show villain. "But I just got a text from my mom. She made food for us already. We've got to go."

"Oh," Sean says, then gives me a smile. "Sorry. See you tomorrow?"

"Sure!" I chirp, then inwardly swat myself for chirping. Still, when I watch him walk away, I'm rewarded by seeing him turn around to smile again. Twice.

Amalita laughs. "So much for stealth. You are on that girl's list."

I look at her. "What do you mean?"

"Did you not see Reenzie's death glare? She's going to make your life miserable."

38

"Why?" I ask, feeling nervous. "What did I do?"

Amalita links her arm with mine and starts to walk me through the mall. "She's in love with Sean. Everyone knows it except him. Or maybe he does, but he must not be into her."

I find myself hoping he is really, really not into her.

"Sean likes keeping everything peaceful and no-conflict," she carries on. "Like asking us to dinner. He's not an idiot; he knows about me and Tee and Reenzie. He knows it's not going to happen."

"So he didn't mean it?"

I try not to sound anxious, but Amalita grins, and I know I do.

"Oh, no, he wanted us to come. Or more specifically, he wanted *you* to come." She lets out a bitter laugh. "He's just one of those people who think if you ignore the awful stuff, it'll all go away."

I consider that for a second. "That's . . . kind of sweet."

"You think?" Amalita didn't look convinced. "You can close your eyes to a problem, but when you open them, it's still there, whether you want it there or not."

▼

Unlike Sean and his crew, Amalita and I do hit the food court, but we opt out of Blackbeard's in favor of chili cheese fries, combining vegetables, dairy, and protein into the perfect, well-rounded meal. I'm not all that hungry when I get home, although the enchiladas Mom made for dinner smell ridiculously delicious.

"How was school?" she asks, looking up from her tablet.

"It was great," I say. I pour myself a glass of water, then rummage through the pantry, looking for a dessert I can take up to my room for later.

"I'm glad," Mom says. "I know it was a tough morning."

"Mm-hmm." Found it. Chocolate graham crackers.

"Do you have a second?" she asks. "I need to talk to you."

There's something in her voice I don't like. I sit across from her at the kitchen table.

"I want you to hear something." She gets up and presses a button on the answering machine. A reedy, Cuban-accented voice plays out of it.

"Autumn, *mi corazón*, it's Eddy, your grandmother. Your mother promised me she'd play this for you if I called back. I need to see you, *querida*. I miss you, but it's not just that. I have something *muy importante* for you. Something that could change your life."

There's an extended breathy silence, as if she wasn't sure how to end the message; then the phone beeps into silence.

" '*Eddy, your grandmother*'?" I say.

"I know. And I know she's a little dramatic. But we've been in Florida three weeks. I visit Eddy almost every day. Erick comes with me at least twice a week. You've gone once. *Once.*"

"I've been busy!"

Mom looks at me like that's the most exasperating thing I've ever said.

"Plus, she's crazy," I add when Mom doesn't lose the stare. "I know she had a stroke and she can't help it, but listen to her: 'something that could change your life'? Who says that?"

"Can I tell you what I think?" Mom asks in her handling-with-kid-gloves voice. "I think you blame Eddy for what happened to Daddy."

Really? Is that supposed to be some kind of psychological breakthrough?

"Of course it's her fault," I say. "If she hadn't gotten sick, Dad wouldn't have been down here and he wouldn't have gotten in the accident. That's just a fact."

Mom looks surprised. "Okay. But it's nothing she intended. You can't blame her for it."

Pretty sure I can, but all of a sudden I'm so tired I can't keep my eyes open. I need to get upstairs, so I promise Mom I'll go see Eddy tomorrow after school. I'll stay long enough to get whatever life-changing wonder she has to give me, then get out of there.

I can all but guarantee the life-changing gift will be a new ceramic pot.

5

I leave early for school the next day. I'll be the first to get to the spot where J.J. and I converged, hang out until *he* falls into step behind *me,* then wheel around on him and tell him stalking is a federal offense punishable by life in prison without possibility of anagrams. I even giggle to myself as I turn the corner and near the side street where he emerged yesterday, because there's no sign of him up ahead.

Until he steps casually out of a hedge and falls into step right next to me.

"You really shouldn't walk too close to these bushes," he says. "You never know what secrets they conceal."

He actually scared the hell out of me, but I manage to sound cool despite my thumping heart.

"This is what we do now?" I ask, secretly overjoyed that I have a friend to walk with.

"It could be," he says, brushing shrub off his body as we

walk, "but unless I blow off all my other work and start building evil-genius-worthy plans with detailed blueprints, I'm going to run out of interesting ways to cross your path in about five days."

"You have five more days mapped out?"

"Which I'd like to save for special surprise occasions. Halloween, maybe, or your birthday. Neither of which I'll actually use since I mentioned them and they'd no longer be surprises. Unless I'm just saying I won't to throw you off. Which I'm not. Or *am* I?"

"How about I just text you when I leave in the morning so you know when to meet me?"

"Better." We exchange numbers.

"Your head looks better," he notices. "Less—"

I hold up a hand. "No need to elaborate. Thanks."

When we get to school, J.J. and I branch off to our lockers, but mine won't open.

I figure I dialed the combination wrong. I try it again. Nothing. I yank harder.

J.J. comes back. Jack's with him now, showing J.J. something on his phone. "Article, *New York Times*," Jack says. "Mainstream frickin' media. 'Comic-Obsessed? You Are the New Cool.'"

"Bull," J.J. says.

I now have one foot against my locker, I'm holding the combination lock, and I'm leaning back as hard as I can. If it does open, I'm going to go sprawling. I feel the prickle of flop sweat under my arms.

"You guys, I can't get this open."

"Did you dial the combination right?" Jack asks.

"Oh, right, I should have thought of that," I say sarcastically. "I dialed it right *six times*. It won't open."

"Let me try," J.J. offers. I let him take my place, then read him off the numbers. He dials them slowly, and then, in a sudden burst, he yanks down hard on the combination lock.

"Ow! I think I sprained my shoulder!"

Jack and I laugh while J.J. bounces back, shaking out his arm.

"Seriously?" he says to me. "I was doing that for you!"

"I know. I'm sorry," I say, trying to compose myself. "You were just so cool about the whole thing, and then—"

"Hey!" Amalita marches down the hall in a bright purple stretchy dress and turquoise chandelier earrings. "Where have you people been? I've been out on the lawn by myself."

"Autumn broke her lock," Jack says.

"I didn't break it, it won't open," I say.

"Leave it," she says. "We've got to get to class."

Sure enough, the halls are emptying around us. I'm starting to sweat again. "I can't. My French textbook is in there. This is the only time I can get it between now and second period."

"It's okay," J.J. says. "We'll cut off the lock."

I have no idea how he intends to do that, but he stays with me while Amalita and Jack head off to homeroom. In the end, J.J. doesn't actually cut the lock, but he does find the janitor. The man is watching TV in the custodial lounge and takes his own sweet time meandering down the hall, dragging a massive pair of bolt-cutters. The actual snipping takes about a second, after which I grab my books, say good-bye to J.J., and race down the hall to homeroom.

Late again, and this time a sweaty mess. Naturally, Sean is one of the many people who wheel around to get a good look.

"Autumn Falls . . . short of the mark again?" Ms. Knowles reads off the attendance sheet as I slip into the one open seat. It's in the back row, but as everyone laughs at the oh-so-clever quip, Reenzie Tresca spins around in her seat.

And winks.

And I get it.

"She changed my lock," I tell Amalita, J.J., and Jack at lunch. I take an angry bite of my cheese sandwich.

"I told you, you're on her list," Amalita says, shrugging.

"It's possible," J.J. says between bites of his pork roll. "She'd have had to come to school late yesterday or early today, snip off your lock, and put on a new one."

"Usually they dumb-lock people. It gets old," Jack says as he scrolls through Instagram photos.

"But I didn't do anything. How come you're not on her list?" I ask Amalita. "You're in her face all the time."

"She stole my best friend," Amalita says vehemently. "*She's* on *my* list."

"What is it with these people and lists?" Jenna asks me later when I call her. School's over and I'm on the bus that will take me to Eddy's place. I considered blowing it off, but I promised, so I'll go. Briefly.

"I don't know," I say as the bus passes a cherry-red Porsche with a Maltese hanging out the window. "You and I never had lists. No one we knew had lists. Now it's like *Scarface*. They're very vengeful here."

"Must be the humidity," Jenna says. We talk for a few minutes and then I realize I'm at my stop and we say good-bye.

The bus lets me out right in front of Century Acres. Despite its name, the place doesn't sprawl over acres of land. It's big, but it's a single building, with high ceilings and three floors of apartments that branch off from the main lobby in two long wings.

When I walk inside, I'm assaulted by piano music. The lobby opens up to a spacious lounge, with couches plus rows of folding chairs. Every seat is filled, and elderly men and women smile and clap in time to the jangling music and the off-key but enthusiastic voice of a male singer belting out a medley of old standards.

I scan the white heads. From the back, any one of them could be Eddy.

Then I hear the voice. She's crooning along with the singer, her heavy Cuban accent mangling every other word.

No. Way.

My eighty-year-old, pink-tracksuit-wearing grand-mother is sprawled across the piano on her stomach, stretching to reach the microphone as she kicks her purple sneakers in the air. She presses her cheek against the middle-aged balding guy with Einstein-wild hair who's playing the piano, and together they belt out the chorus.

"Everybody sing!" she shouts, sitting up. She holds her arms high above her head and sways from side to side.

That's it. I'm out of here.

"Autumn!" she cries.

Crap. I haven't even made it two steps.

"Eddy!" I say through the smile plastered on my face. "I didn't see you up there."

Eddy grabs the microphone. "Ladies and gentlemen, my granddaughter, Autumn! She has the voice of an angel! Come sing with us, Autumn!"

The whole room applauds. Why did I agree to come here?

I make my way to Eddy and she shoves the microphone in my face. "Hi, everyone," I say, giving a wan smile. "I'm, um, not going to sing. I just came here to visit my grand-mother."

There's a chorus of "Awwwws" and one angry "Then get off the stage!"

"Oh, be quiet," Eddy snaps at the heckler. She slides off the piano, then takes my hand and snakes us through the crowd. She only comes up to my chest, but she's fast; I practically have to run to keep up with her.

She slows down once we're in the open hall and on our way to her room. She wraps her arm around me and pulls me close, which smushes her head into the side of my boob. It's a little disconcerting.

"Hi, Mrs. Rubenstein!" Eddy calls to a woman shuffling our way. The two of them hug and chat about their families, Eddy introduces me . . . then the minute we start walking again Eddy mutters, "The woman's a pill. Switched bingo cards with me two weeks in a row. And mine was a winner."

She doesn't say this softly. I look over my shoulder to apologize, but Mrs. Rubenstein has the same smile on her face as before.

Two conclusions: (1) High school never ends, and (2) It's more pleasant when you can't hear the awful things people say.

Maybe I should invest in earplugs.

I've pretty much had my fill of Century Acres by the time we get to Eddy's room and she settles into her favorite chair, but she's in the middle of another story. "And the nurses," she says, "the meds they give me? Not what my doctor ordered." She lowers her voice to a whisper even though there's no one else in the room and the door's closed. "They're running experiments."

I reach into my bag for my phone, wondering if Eddy will notice if I text Jenna.

"You tried to make him the *boniatillo*," Eddy says. "He **would have loved that.**"

I freeze midreach. "What?"

Eddy leans forward in her chair. Her wrinkled brown face is solemn and her eyes are sad.

"Reinaldo. The day he was coming home. It was a good choice. It was always his favorite. Just like you were. Don't tell your brother I said so, though."

She winks at me, but I'm having a tough time following. Which is ironic, since this is the first thing she's said that makes any sense.

"Mom told you about that?"

"Your brother. He showed me a little movie of you. A chef you're not, *mi corazón,* but by the end it looked *muy delicioso, muy auténtico.*"

"Thanks."

My voice is barely a whisper. Mom, Erick, and I never talk about that day. Ever.

"You heard my message?" she asks.

I nod. "You have something for me that will change my life?"

"If you let it."

Eddy pulls something out of her night-table drawer and hands it to me. It's a paper napkin folded around something rectangular. "Sorry about the wrapping. Reinaldo gave it to me before he left. I didn't have anything else to put it in."

Inside the napkin is a brown leather journal. The cover is embossed with a symbol that looks like a triangle with a face in it. I rub my thumb over it. The whole cover feels soft

49

and weathered, but when I flip it open I see that the crisp, lined pages are blank and clean.

"Dad gave this to you?" I ask.

"To pass on to you."

I shake my head. "He was on his way home. If he wanted to give it to me, why didn't he have it with him?"

Eddy shifts back into her chair with a painfully sad sigh. "Your father . . . knew things."

"Like what? Are you saying he knew he was going to get into an accident?" Eddy doesn't answer. "No," I say, trying to keep my voice calm. "If he knew, he wouldn't have gotten into the car. He'd have stayed at the hotel."

"I don't know how it worked, *querida*. I don't know what he could or couldn't change. I only know what he told me. To give this to you. To let you know it could change your life."

"It's a journal," I say, waving it in the air. "How is that going to change my life?"

She wraps her arms around her bony body. "Do you feel that? They turned down the temperature. They do that here. They never want us to get too comfortable."

Uh-oh. I'm losing her. "Eddy, what did Dad say? Specifically. How did he say a journal would change my life?"

Eddy suddenly bolts forward and grabs my wrist. "Write in it, Autumn."

Ow. She's eighty years old. How can she have a grip of steel? Must be from all that pottery.

"Promise me," she insists.

"Okay, okay. I'll write in it."

"Wonderful," she says. "Now help me pick out a dress. There's a Sadie Hawkins dance, and if I don't ask Juan-Carlos *esta tarde,* Dariana will get to him first."

"Juan-Carlos . . . Falciano?" I ask carefully.

"*Sí.* You know him?"

Not really, but I do know he was my grandfather. Daddy started going by "Falls" in college. "Yeah," I assure her, "he's a catch. I bet he'll totally go to the dance with you."

Eddy beams. I spend the next half hour helping her get dressed and ready for a man who's been dead forty years; then I say good-bye.

I have some writing to do.

6

I intend to sit down on a bench outside Century Acres to write in the journal, but something is bothering me, so I don't do it. I wait until I get on the bus, then text Jenna the whole story.

> **AUTUMN:** What do you think, real or delusional?

> **JENNA:** Y would your dad torture you?
> DELUSIONAL!

She's right. I hate writing, and Dad knew it. It's a dyslexia thing; words don't come out the way I want them to. Why would he give me something I'd have to trudge through hell to use?

My phone chirps.

> **JENNA:** Unless . . . is there a note?

I didn't check. Why didn't I check? Of course if he was going to give me something as twisted as a journal, he'd leave a note to tell me why.

I pull out the book and turn each page slowly.

AUTUMN: No note.

JENNA: Mystery solved. Journal = Eddy's gift 2 you, not your dad's, but E messed in head & confused.

AUTUMN: Yeah. OK.

JENNA: You should use it tho.

AUTUMN: ?!?!?!?

JENNA: You can use journal for an anti-list. A wish list for good.

AUTUMN: Maybe . . . still involves writing. ☹

She's right about Eddy. Of course she is. Eddy was nuts even before she had her stroke. Now she's over the edge. If what she said was true, that would mean Dad knew he was going to die and couldn't do anything about it.

Horrific.

But if he *did* know he was going to die . . . and if he *couldn't* do anything about it . . . it would be pretty cool to have one last gift from him. Even a random gift he'd never expect me to use.

"Hey, Mom," I ask during dinner, "did Dad ever . . . sense things?"

"Oh God," she groans. "What did Eddy tell you?"

"Sense things?" Erick asks. "Like ESP?"

"She didn't tell me anything," I say, taking a sip of milk. "She just . . . you know . . . hinted."

Erick puts his hands to his temples. "I sense that Schmidt is going to beg for meat loaf." Sure enough, Schmidt starts to whine. "It's inherited. I'm a genius."

"You're a loser," I say. "He's been doing that since we sat down."

"Your grandmother always had some wild ideas, even before the stroke," Mom says. "You can't believe them. Your father was gifted in a million ways, but not the way Eddy likes to think."

I let it go. But when I go up to my room, I take out the journal and flop down with it on my bed. I stare at the triangle face on the front. It's such a strange image. It looks like a child could have scrawled it, but it's intricate too. Like hieroglyphics.

I pull open the cover. Nothing special inside at all. If I searched hard enough I probably could find this exact same journal at the mall. Most likely that's where Eddy found it, on a Century Acres bus trip.

Still . . .

I grab a pen.

I don't want to keep a diary. I'm not the diary type.

Jenna's wish-list idea doesn't seem right either. There's only one reason I'm even interested in this journal, so there's really only one thing it feels right to do.

Dear Dad,

I know you're not connected to this thing, and it's not like you can actually read it, but I miss you. A lot. So much I'm even willing to write. I know. I'm guessing you feel extremely honored. . . .

I always write slowly, so it takes forever, and I can pretty much guarantee that ninety percent of the words are spelled wrong, but I tell him everything. I write more than I've ever written in my life.

It feels good.

It shouldn't. It's a journal, not my dad, and part of me feels like a sap for getting so into it . . . but screw it, I like writing to him. When I feel like I've said everything I want to say, I think again about Jenna's wish list idea. This time it makes me smile and I add one last sentence.

I wish just one thing here could be easy.

I close the book and feel absolutely fantastic for exactly one minute . . . until I look at the clock.

It's midnight and I haven't even started my homework.

I am an idiot.

I might be a prophetic idiot, though, because over the next two weeks, *exactly* one thing is easy. I have a pop quiz in French that I hard-core ace because it's all oral conversations in front of the class. No writing at all.

The rest of my life? A giant ball of stress.

Classes at Aventura are a million times harder than the ones at Stillwater, and there's so much reading that I'm up late into the night, every night. Amalita and J.J. have been great. One or both of them usually hangs out with me after school, and we all work together either at the outdoor courtyard at the mall or at one of our houses. Jack sometimes hangs too, but he's distracting because he's apparently some kind of supergenius. He finishes everything while he's still in class, so while we're all trying to work, he's quoting his favorite panels from whatever comic he's reading.

As for the journal, I don't have time to write anything as long as my first entry. I carry it with me, though, just in case I have a second to jot something down. I'm fully aware that carrying a journal is a prime setup for disaster, but I can't help it. It makes me feel good to keep it close.

There's one other thing that has me stressed out, and I finally bring it up one day at lunch.

"Check it out," I say. "She's staring at me."

"She who?" J.J. asks.

"She *Reenzie*."

They all follow my gaze across the field and look right at her.

"Stop it!" I hiss.

"Yeah," Jack says. "You don't want to look her in the eye or you'll turn to stone."

"A Medusa reference," J.J. says. "Impressive. You read that in a Greek mythology comic book?"

"Bite me," Jack says as he checks out a pretty girl with blond pigtails walking by us.

"*Dios mío,*" Amalita mutters. "What's the problem, Autumn? She's giving you the *mal de ojo*? Let me talk to her." She gets to her feet and shouts "Hey!" before I yank her back down.

"Stop! You'll make it worse. It's not a huge deal," I say. "It's just that she's *always* doing that, looking at me like she wants to kill me. Ever since that day in the mall."

"When she realized her man wants you," Amalita says.

"But Sean's not her man," I say. "You told me he's not into her."

"And we have no way of knowing he wants Autumn," J.J. points out. "He didn't ask you out or anything, did he?"

Jack snorts.

"No," I say. "He's nice to me. He talks to me when I see him in homeroom. We'll walk together a little on our way to our next class sometimes. That's it."

"Which is nothing," J.J. says.

"Unless he talks about you in front of Reenzie," Amalita says.

"Whatever," J.J. says. "I think you should let it go. She wants to glare, let her glare. You're stressed-out enough with work and life and stuff that actually matters. Don't let Reenzie Tresca add to it. She's not worth it."

"You're right," I say. "Except . . . I feel like she's plotting something."

And then lunch ends and I think about it in chemistry class and I'm freaked out all over again. I excuse myself to the bathroom and bring my bag, then duck into an empty science lab. I yank out the journal and scribble as quickly as I can:

Dear Dad,

Something's been bugging me and I think I'll feel better about it if I just tell you.

I let him know how anxious I am, and for the first time since that beginning entry I end with something on the wish list.

I wish that if Reenzie were going to do something to me she'd just go ahead and do it so I wouldn't have to wait.

I close the book and take a deep breath.

I feel better.

The rest of the day flies by. After school it's homework, then dinner, then a little TV before I go up to my room to slog through more of my endless reading assignments.

The text from Amalita comes in at eleven.

If you're up, it says, DO NOT log on to the student portal.

So of course I do.

Oh. My. God.

7

The Aventura High student portal is like most student portals. You log on with your name and password, click on your class year, and get to a page where teachers post long-term assignments, reference guides, study materials, announcements . . . administrative stuff.

At least, that's usually what you find. This time when I log on and click on the sophomore class page, I'm greeted by a full-screen image of *me.*

It's a close-up of my face, and it must have been taken my first day of school, because the giant cleft lump swells mountainously out of my forehead. I obviously have no idea the picture is being taken. My lips are oddly puckered and my eyelids are half closed. I'm sure I was in the middle of saying something, but the shot makes it look like I'm in the throes of ecstasy. The focus is soft, like the picture was snapped from far away and blown up, but there's no doubt at all it's me.

I click everywhere and press every button on the keyboard, but it doesn't go away.

I'm shaking. I want to call Amalita, but it's far too late, so I text her back.

AUTUMN: I'm gonna kill her.

AMALITA: I told you not to look.

AUTUMN: Maybe they'll pull it down before
people see it?

AMALITA: I heard from Carrie Amernick.
Mass email. Too late.

I have no clue what to do with myself. I'm so furious I'm still shaking. I should close the screen, but I don't. My hideous face keeps staring at me.

What the heck do I do? I could wake up Mom. *That* wouldn't be mortifying at all.

I have to move. I feel as if my nerves are on fire and I can't sit still. I pace around my room in circles, climbing over the bed each lap as though it's a giant hurdle. I actually laugh out loud when I think how badly I *wanted* Reenzie to just go ahead and do whatever she was going to do. I even wrote it to Dad in the journal. Careful what you wish for, right?

I close the link to get rid of my hideous face. I log back on to the school website, but instead of the portal I click on the disciplinary policy and scroll down to "harassment."

The punishment ranges from detention to an alternative disciplinary school.

So if all goes well, when Mrs. Dorio finds out Reenzie posted the picture, she'll be in a far bigger world of hurt than I could ever put her in.

I send Jenna the link with my log-in information and the word REVENGE all in caps. Somehow I get to sleep that night, and I wake up to my phone ringing.

"Hello?"

"Reality check." It's Jenna. "Yes, it's a horrible picture, and Reenzie is a horrible human being for posting it. But seriously? You're not naked, you're not doing anything illegal, you just look kind of dopey. Right now, she gets caught, she's in trouble. You go for revenge, you're the one in trouble and your life gets completely messed up. She's not worth it."

"I know." For whatever reason, I'm not as upset as I was last night. "You're right. I'll let it go."

"Not let it go," Jenna corrects me, "complain about it. Then let the people handle it who are supposed to handle it."

"Agreed. Love you."

"Love you more."

I don't say anything to Mom or Erick about the picture, though I know I'm depriving my loving brother. He'd click on the screen and think it was Christmas all over again.

When I meet J.J. at our corner on the way to school, he opens his mouth but nothing comes out.

"I've seen it," I tell him, saving him the trouble.

"So . . . you okay?"

"Now I am," I say, and realize that it's not a lie, that I actually *do* feel okay. "Last night, not so much. The stupidest part is Reenzie's doing this because of *Sean*. It's not like he and I are even together."

"Tell her that."

I roll my eyes. "Pretty sure she knows."

"Make it clear," J.J. says. "Come right out and tell Reenzie you're not at all into Sean. Tell her you have no desire to go out with him and wouldn't even if he asked you. Then maybe she'll get it and leave you alone."

"Okay," I say slowly, "but then what if he did ask me out and I wanted to say yes?"

"Would you?"

"Maybe. I like Sean. I mean, I *could* like Sean. I don't really know him well enough to say."

We get to school, and the whispers and laughs start the minute we walk in the door. Not just sophomores either; apparently everyone got the memo to check out the portal.

People have too much time on their hands.

"We need to bring her down," Amalita says, shaking her head when she sees me. "And don't worry, I've watched every episode of *Pretty Little Liars*. I have ideas."

"No revenge," I say. "Let the school get her in trouble."

"What if they don't catch her?" Amalita asks. "Her brother's at MIT. Computer nerd. Supersmart. What if he made sure she can't get caught?"

I'm at my locker now, and there's an envelope sticking out between the slats. I open it, then flash it at Amalita and J.J.

"Mrs. Dorio wants to see me," I say smugly. "First nail in Reenzie's coffin."

"Nailing her in a coffin's on my list too," Amalita says. "Think about it."

What I think is that I never want Amalita on my bad side.

I feel good walking into Mrs. Dorio's office. I remember my first day, the way she reeled off all the expellable offenses as though she was just dying to put the smackdown on some wayward student. She's probably loving this. Most likely she already knows Reenzie did it and just wants me to help build the case against her.

She shuts the door behind me and leans against the front of her desk. "So tell me," she says, "is this something you did to get attention?"

"What?" Her question's so ridiculous I feel like that should be answer enough, but Mrs. Dorio's clearly looking for more.

"No," I say, trying to stay calm. "I didn't do it for *any* reason. I'm not the one who did it."

I'm so outraged I want to scream, but I hold it together while Mrs. Dorio stares me down like she's waiting for me to crack. Finally she sighs. "I believe you. I just had to check."

"Why?" I ask. "You don't know who did it? You can't tell? You can't, I don't know . . . trace who uploaded it?"

"We're looking into it. You can go back to class." She sits down at her desk and starts to shuffle through papers.

That can't be it. This can't be over.

"Don't you want to know who *I* think did it?" I ask, dying to tell my side of the story.

Mrs. Dorio leans back in her chair. "Here's the deal. I would very much like to know who you think did it, but I won't be able to act on it unless we have proof. It's a school-district policy, Autumn. If I go after a student without adequate proof, *I'm* the one with harassment charges from angry parents. So before you tell me who you think did it, do you have proof?"

"No," I admit, my shoulders slumping. "But I know who did it."

"I don't doubt you do, and it would be lovely if that were enough. But it's not. We'll look for proof on our end, and if you find anything you let me know. In the meantime, the picture's down and we're changing our passwords so this won't happen again. Thank you, Autumn."

She looks back down at her desk. I haven't even left the room yet, but clearly I'm already gone.

So there it is. Reenzie's going to get away with it. Guaranteed that if the tables were turned and I was the one who posted the picture of her, they'd know it was me within the hour.

I'm so furious I want to scream, but that would only make it worse. It's still homeroom; I should go, but I refuse to walk in late so everyone can stare. Not today. Instead I take my bag outside and huddle on the grass with my back against the school. I'm right under the windows; no one could see me if they tried. I pull out the journal.

Dear Dad, I write.

No offense, but Aventura officially sucks.

I scrawl out the whole story, finishing with the same stuff I told J.J.—that it's especially frustrating to be targeted over a guy who, yes, is obscenely hot, but who I might not even like. I'm still angry afterward, but it's less overwhelming once I get it down on paper. Then I pick up my pen to add one more thing.

You know what I really wish? I wish I had the chance to at least hang out with Sean. Just so I'd know if he's worth the trouble.

I hear the roar of everyone leaving homeroom and quickly tuck my journal back in my bag before I join the masses and head to class.

After fourth period, I find another envelope sticking out of my locker. I'm hoping it's from Mrs. Dorio, saying they found proof Reenzie posted the picture, but no. It's a reminder that I'm supposed to skip my afternoon classes and spend those hours in ADAPT, which of course I'd completely forgotten.

"Isn't that the short-bus class?" Jack asks when I mention it at lunch.

"*You're* the short-bus class," J.J. retorts, shoving him.

"Rude!" I snap. "ADAPT is *not* the short-bus class. It's the Gimp Squad."

"See!" Jack exploded. "Now *you're* rude!"

"I can make fun of it," I say. "You can't."

"What's it about?" Amalita says. "The . . . whatever I'm allowed to call it."

"ADAPT," I say. "Aventura's Developmental Advancement Program for Teens. I went to one like it at my old school too. It's all about coping skills for people with different learning disabilities. You know how I always listen to the *Hamlet* audiobook while I'm reading it? That's a Gimp Squad trick."

"I like Gimp Squad," Jack says. "Makes you sound like the Justice League with issues."

"I don't know," I say. "A special school for teens with unique abilities . . . sounds more X-Men to me."

"You know she could pull off the outfit," Jack continues to J.J. "Old-school, from the comic. Thigh-high boots, green-and-yellow bodysuit that hugs up the boobs . . ."

" 'Hugs up the boobs'?" J.J. asks. "What are you, twelve?"

"I'm going to go," I say, standing up. "Do me a favor and don't say anything about ADAPT. It's not like it's a big deal, but—"

"*No es nada.*" Amalita waves me away. "Go."

I smile as I bus my tray. I like that I already have friends who get it without me having to explain. It's not like I'm ashamed of my dyslexia or anything, but people here are already talking behind my back. I don't need to give them more ammunition.

ADAPT's in Aventura High's black box theater, which means nothing to me until I walk in and see it's an actual black box of a room, including black chairs and a black stage.

Until now I didn't think it was possible to feel any paler. My arm looks like it glows.

"Autumn! Hey."

It's Sean. He's sitting in one of the seats.

"You're ADAPT too?" he asks.

He's smiling like he's happy to see me, so I slip into the seat next to him. "Yeah. Dyslexia. What's your damage?"

"Auditory Processing Disorder."

"Fancy name."

"I'm a fancy guy. But when there's a lot of background noise I have trouble picking out words and understanding them. Unless I focus very hard."

He slowly leans forward until his face is an inch from mine. Even this close he looks incredible. My heart pounds. He could kiss me. He could kiss me right now. Our lips are a breath apart.

"Teachers like it when you look at them like that?" I say it casually, like I'm not about to hyperventilate.

"They love it."

I love it too. It's painful when he sits back in his seat, but the room is almost full and some older guy just stepped onstage, so I guess things are about to start.

For all the crap I gave it, the Gimp Squad at home was kind of amazingly helpful, and I have my doubts that ADAPT will be as good. Turns out it's pretty terrific. They break us up into groups sorted by Gimptitude. Mine's run by Evan, a rail-thin Asian biker chick with a tongue stud and a pink streak in her hair who's apparently both dyslexic and an honors grad student at FIU. She clues us in on her favorite tip: soft sandpaper. Every time she learns a new word she writes it on the sandpaper and presses hard enough to make an imprint. After she *feels* the word, says it out loud, and writes it again, she swears she never gets it mixed up again.

Evan's the bad-ass Miracle Worker. I like her.

ADAPT technically ends at the close of the school day, but they let us out about a half hour early. I hang in the black box while Sean finishes talking to his own group leader. The second he's done I casually slide out beside him.

"So how'd you adapt to ADAPT?" he asks.

"Far better than I'm adapting to you as a guy who tells corny jokes."

He smiles. "Come with me."

"Demanding much?" I ask, though the truth is if he keeps smiling like that I will follow him anywhere.

"Demanded *of*," he says. "Three older brothers. That's why I like playing quarterback. Lets me give orders to someone else."

"Wow," I say. "How hard did you have to work that answer to slip in that you play quarterback?"

"I'm exhausted from the effort," he says. "Are you duly impressed?"

"Swooning."

"I like that," he says. "It's rare I get a good swoon."

We're at the far end of campus now, wandering by the athletic fields, and I'm surprised how much I like talking to him.

"You're different than I thought you'd be," I admit. I mean it as a compliment. I knew he was nice and polite, but until now I worried his personality stopped there.

"You thought I was what, quieter? Maybe not so quick?"

I shrug, feeling like he caught me. "Kind of."

"It's okay. I get that sometimes. It's the Auditory Processing thing. I miss stuff, especially in big groups, and default to smile-and-nod. I like to think I'm better one-on-one."

I remember what Amalita said about him, that instead of dealing with difficult situations he ignores them and hopes they'll go away. She still might be right, but now I wonder if part of that is him not always knowing the bad stuff exists.

"So what's the deal with you and J.J. Austin?" he asks, switching topics. "Are you guys together?"

"Me and J.J.? For real?" I blink at him in surprise.

Sean shrugs. "I see you together all the time. I just thought . . ."

"We're friends," I say more quickly than I probably should.

I suck in my cheeks so I don't grin. Sean's checking up on my status. He's been watching me to see if I'm available.

69

"How about you and Reenzie?" I ask.

Sean smiles. "Our parents have been best friends since college, we've lived next door to each other our whole lives, and when I look at her I still see an eight-year-old girl."

I give him a dubious look. "Really," I say flatly.

He nods. "She's like my sister. I had to make out with her on a dare once at a party. It felt like kissing my brother."

I consider asking how exactly he'd know how kissing his brother feels, but I like his answer too much to mess with it.

Across the campus, I see dots of people emerge from the main building. Class is officially over. We automatically start walking back toward our lockers.

"Are you around for the next couple hours?" Sean asks. "I have track, but you could hang and watch practice if you want. Maybe we could hang out after."

"That would be great," I say.

Amazing. I wanted time with Sean and I got it. Now I know.

I like him. A lot.

Guess I'll be staying on Reenzie's list.

Shauna

Autumn falls

Book
Mark

8

Almost feels like home, I text Jenna. Walking down to watch track practice.

I used to watch Jenna's practices from time to time. It's the same scene, except here there's a huge grassy hill leading down to the track, and everyone is sprawled out on it. In Maryland, only the athletes got soaked in sweat, while in Florida, the air is so thick and sticky that after two minutes I can wring out my skin.

I'm not the only one sitting by myself, but just about. I didn't tell my friends I was coming. Sean asked *me*. It would have felt lame showing up with a posse.

The good thing is no one seems to care. No stares, no snickers. Jenna was right: the picture was embarrassing, but one bad picture offers only limited entertainment. The world has moved on.

I look around for Sean, but both the boys' and girls' teams practice together, and there are groups everywhere doing sprints and hurdles. The field in the middle is covered too—people stretching, long-jumping, pole-vaulting . . .

Unbelievable. Marina Tresca is pole-vaulting. I can't escape this girl. As I watch, she races forward, plants her pole into the dirt, and hurls herself impossibly high into the air. She sails over the bar with so much room to spare that all the other pole-vaulters applaud.

So the wench who's out to humiliate me isn't just evil, she's an evil ninja. Perfect.

She hasn't seen me yet. I should go before she does. It's not running away, it's avoiding unnecessary hell.

"Autumn!"

It's Sean, and Reenzie and I both turn when he calls my name. He smiles at me before he joins his teammates on the ground. They're doing core work. Planks. His arms tense as they hold his body taut, and I have to wrap my own arms around my knees so I don't race onto the field and touch the rigid outline of his bicep.

I might be drooling. If I'm going to come out here regularly I might need to bring a bib. I hold up my phone and pretend to check messages while I zoom in and take a picture to text to Jenna. I send it with no message. It speaks for itself.

I planned to do homework while I was down here, but it's far more entertaining to watch Sean sprint. The boy is hard-core rocking the shorts and singlet. He's fast, and when his arms and legs pump down the field, every muscle on his perfectly tanned body ripples and flexes and . . .

He's like a jungle panther, I text Jenna.

If you're lucky, maybe he'll pounce, she replies.

Sadly, the one who looks ready to pounce is Reenzie. She keeps glaring at me like I'm dinner, and I'm fairly certain fire actually flares out of her eyes when Sean ambles over between sprints and collapses on the ground next to me.

Ignore the witch. Jungle panther in near proximity.

"Thanks for hanging out," Sean says, taking a swig from his water bottle.

"You *should* thank me," I say, adjusting my ponytail. "It's hard sitting out here in the hot sun. It's a serious aerobic workout."

"'Cause your heart is pounding so fast watching me run?"

"Yeah, that's it, stud." I laugh. "You're pretty fast."

He laughs too and bends forward into a hamstring stretch. "Oh, yeah? Who've you been talking to?"

"Running," I clarify. "Fast *running*."

"I'm not. I mean, I'm okay, but football's more my thing."

"Right, someone told me you play quarterback. Oh, wait, that was you."

I could keep this up all day, but Sean has to go back to the track. I won't even look at Reenzie; she's probably lancing a voodoo doll of me with her pole.

More likely she's planning her next online assault. I heard they were reviewing the school portal with some sort of hacker prevention team, but that will just make Reenzie more creative. She'll make a fake Facebook account with my name, or a Pinterest page filled with pictures that'll make last night's look flattering.

I hate this. I hate that I have to worry about what Reenzie's going to do. I hate that I can't just enjoy seeing whatever happens with Sean without having to watch my back.

Forget it. I'll enjoy it *and* I'll watch my back. And if she does anything else, I'll make sure she gets caught. I feel so determined about it that I pull the journal from my bag.

Dear Dad, I begin.

I refuse to let Marina Tresca change the way I live my life. She won't get away with anything else, but she is otherwise completely meaningless to me.

I chew my pen for a second, thinking, then add:

It would still be awesome to see her wipe out right here in front of me. I wish she'd slip and fall and her pole would split.

I tuck my journal away in the bag and go back to watching Sean. I've had boyfriends who played sports before, but I've never been the girlfriend-in-the-stands type. Only for Jenna, but she'd put in the hours. She'd earned my devotion.

Sean, though . . . I could handle being watch-from-the-stands girl for him. I could even enjoy it.

"Are you kidding me?"

The shriek is bloodcurdling. I snap to its direction and

see Reenzie slowly getting to her feet. Goose bumps race across my skin. From the way she screamed I assume she broke something, and here I was wishing for her to wipe out. But no, she's not limping. She's filthy. She's streaked with mud and holds her arms far from her body and her legs bowed like all her limbs are badly sunburned and she doesn't want them to touch anything. Walking that way she looks stiff, but not hurt. Teammates—including Sean—flock toward her, but quickly pull back to a wide diameter.

"Just get away from me!" she screams.

Some back away, but a circle of girls walks with her off the field and toward the locker room. I watch the spectacle until Sean appears next to me.

"What happened to her?" I ask.

"Not sure," he says. "Do you mind if we hang out some other time?"

"Yeah, of course," I say, as if I'm not jealous and a little dubious about the she's-a-sister-to-me thing.

"Great. Give me your phone."

I do and he enters himself in my contacts, then hands it back.

"Text me so I can call you back later. Talk to you soon."

He jogs off in Reenzie's direction. Practice was almost over anyway, and no one's going back to it now. People are still hanging out and talking, but I'm done. I walk home, have dinner with Mom and Erick, and dive into *Hamlet;*

all the while I keep checking my phone to see if Sean will really call.

It's ten at night before he texts me.

SEAN: Hey. Very cool talking w/you today.

AUTUMN: You too. Reenzie OK?

SEAN: Yeah. Pretty bad tho. Someone must have walked their dogs on the field and didn't pick up after them.

AUTUMN: NO!

SEAN: Yeah. Tripped and fell right in it.

AUTUMN: :o

SEAN: BIG dog too. Probably big DOGS.

AUTUMN: ☹

SEAN: I know. Hard-core.

I can't help myself—I screen-shot our text exchange and forward it to Jenna and Amalita, complete with my own LOLs, ☺'s, and huge strings of :D!s. I'm rolling on my bed, laughing so hard I snort, and Erick has to bang on his wall so I'll shut up and he can sleep.

Even after I'm off with Sean, and even after I've called Amalita and relived every detail of Reenzie's in-retrospect-even-more-spectacular wipeout over and over, I'm still not done reveling in it. I pull out the journal so I can record the moment properly, but as I'm about to write I notice the end of my last entry.

I wish she'd slip and fall and her pole would split.

That's what I *thought* I'd written. But now that I see it in front of me, it says something different. I stare at the letters to make sure they're not floating around on me, but the words I see don't change.

I don't know if it was dyslexia or a Freudian slip or a combination of both, but what I *actually* wrote was this:

I wish she'd slip and fall in a pile of shit.

That's graphic.

And specific.

And very eerily accurate.

I flip back to the beginning of my journal. I'm not really looking for anything. There's nothing to find. I'm just curious.

My first entry ended with *I wish just one thing could be easy.*

That's hardly eerie *or* specific. I remember I did have that very easy French quiz a couple days later, but connecting that to a wish for one easy thing is a stretch.

I flip through more journal pages. I remember I wrote a bunch of entries without doing the "I wish" thing, until I wrote

I wish that if Reenzie were going to do something to me she'd just go ahead and do it so I wouldn't have to wait.

My heart stops.

That was just yesterday. And last night Reenzie posted the picture of me on the portal.

My heart's going again, but double time. I flip through more pages to the end of the entry I wrote just this morning, after meeting with Mrs. Dorio.

I wish I had the chance to at least hang out with Sean. Just so I'd know.

What happened after that? I got the letter reminding me about ADAPT, where I got to hang out with Sean.

And then my most recent wish—that Reenzie eat it in a pile of excrement.

I don't realize I'm not breathing until I finally do, and the air sucks in with a long, jagged gasp.

This is why Eddy told me the journal could change my life.

It's a *freaking magic wish-granting journal.*

I have a magic wish-granting journal. I can make anything happen.

My dad *left* me a magic wish-granting journal. He *wanted* me to have the power to make anything happen.

Anything.

I pick up the pen. It shakes in my hand. I have to be very

careful. These are the most important words I'll ever write.

Dear Dad,

Shoot. The tears. I can't cry. I have to write. Deep breath. Okay.

I WISH YOU'D NEVER DIED AND WE ALL LIVED HERE IN AVENTURA TOGETHER, JUST LIKE WE PLANNED.

I sit back and look at the words.

I'm trembling.

What now?

I strain to hear anything. Footsteps. A door opening. Nothing.

This is crazy. I can't sit here all night and wait for something to happen. I'll lose my mind.

I force myself to act like everything's normal. I get ready for bed. I pretend I'm not straining for every click, every swish, every creak, every sound. I crawl under the covers and close my eyes, but they dart around behind my lids.

My stupid brain buzzes unhelpfully with scenes from this stupid horror movie Jenna made me watch with her last summer, but eventually I fall asleep.

I wake up to the sound of my father's voice.

9

"Autumn! Erick! Get your butts down here!"

I bolt awake in a cold sweat, but for a swimmy second I can't imagine why.

"Kids?" Dad calls.

Holy crap.

I jump out of bed, throw open my bedroom door, and race downstairs.

"Dad!" I shout. "Dad!"

I fly into the living room, my heart practically bursting out of my chest . . . and freeze.

Mom and Erick are sitting on the couch with Schmidt sprawled across their laps.

"Look what I've got!" Dad says . . . on the TV. Schmidt's in his arms, but he's just a puppy. I hear Erick and me screaming, then the image spins and it's us on the TV, only Erick's eight and I'm twelve. We run to Dad and he laughs as Schmidt tries to leap out of his arms to get to us.

My face burns and my throat is raw with disappointment. I want to cry. I want to beat my head against the wall for being such an idiot. Instead I say as casually as possible, "You're watching the Schmidt video." Every year Erick watches that video on the anniversary of our getting Schmidt. I can't believe I thought it was really Dad back from the dead.

They don't answer. Mom looks worried, and Erick's staring at me like I'm a car wreck on the side of the road. The disappointment that washes over me is so great I'm not sure I can stand up any longer. I crouch down and give Schmidt a good scratch. "Happy anniversary, pup." I clear my throat. "Could you get me some grapes to bring for lunch?" I ask Mom. "I'm going to go get ready for school."

When I get back to my room I flip through the journal again, and each "wish" I read gets me angrier. How could I have possibly thought the journal was magic? Every single wish can be explained away. Reenzie would have posted the picture of me whether I wished her to or not. ADAPT with Sean was already scheduled, and he was already in it before I even wrote the journal entry. The dog crap thing, yes, that's a weird coincidence, but weird coincidences happen.

Erick's already left for the bus stop by the time I get downstairs. Mom's at the kitchen table reading the newspaper, but she lowers it the second I come in. I know she wants to talk, and it's great that she's there for me and all, but what am I going to do, tell her I'm upset because

I thought I'd brought Dad back from the dead and I hadn't? She'd have me in a psychologist's office within the hour.

"Hi, Mom."

Best to act normal. Normal and busy. No time to stop and talk. I grab a bottle of orange juice and rummage through the pantry and find a granola bar for breakfast.

"Bye, Mom," I call as I head for the door.

"Autumn, please wait." She walks over to me and puts a hand on my shoulder. "This morning . . . are you okay?"

Part of me really wants to tell her. I want her to comfort me and maybe help me feel okay, but there's no way. I'm surprised when the words come tumbling out.

"It was a dream," I say thickly. "I dreamed it never happened, and we'd all moved down here together. It felt so real. And you know how sometimes you wake up and you're still fuzzy and half dreaming? And then I heard his voice, and—"

I can't say any more because I'm starting to cry. Mom pulls me close for a hug, and this time it doesn't matter that she's shorter than I am because for a minute I feel like the smaller one and it feels good.

"I've had those dreams," she says, her own eyes welling up. "Waking up from them is always hard."

I let her hold me a little longer. I may not have told her the exact truth, but the feelings were true, and saying them out loud helped. By the time I say good-bye and head to school I'm much more sane about the whole thing.

"Dirt Cadets . . . Addict Rest . . . Dead Strict . . ."

I'm walking with J.J., and he's making no sense what-soever.

"What are you talking about?" I ask moodily.

"Those are anagrams for 'distracted,'" he says. "What's up?"

He's right. I've said next to nothing our whole walk. I keep wrestling with the journal thing. One second I'm positive all the wishes coming true were pure coincidence, the next I'm wondering all over again. Sure, it didn't bring back my dad, but resurrection's a pretty tall order.

"You're a logical guy, right?" I finally ask J.J.

"I have my Vulcan moments," he says.

"I have no idea what that means."

He sighs. "Yes, I'm a logical guy."

"Do you believe in anything supernatural?" I ask.

"Nope."

"That was a pretty quick answer," I say.

"It's a pretty easy question. Why do you ask?"

"My grandmother," I tell him. Sort-of-truth seems to be working for me today. "She's into a lot of spiritual premo-nitions and life-after-death kinds of things. Weird stuff, but she makes it sound possible, you know?"

"Not really," J.J. says. "I mean, I get that some people believe it, and I don't hold it against them or anything. I'm just more of a debunker."

I drop the subject, at least out loud. I talk to J.J. on autopilot until we get to school. Amalita's already there, pacing in front of my locker.

"Dios mío!" she screams when she sees me. "Do you not check your texts?"

I hadn't this morning. I pull out my phone and see one from Amalita:

OMGOMGOMGOMG!!!!

I nod. "Oh, now I understand . . . absolutely nothing."

"Do you watch *Pop Idol*?" she asks.

"No. My mom and brother love it," I say, "but I'm not into it."

"Me neither. But I *do* follow Kyler Leeds on Twitter, and this morning he announced a contest: Night of Dreams with Kyler Leeds!"

She does a dance to music in her own head, then stops, clearly beside herself at my lack of movement. "Why are you not dancing? This is huge. You watch *Pop Idol,* you go to the Night of Dreams website and answer a question about the show, and you're entered to win, for you and a friend, an actual *night of dreams with Kyler Leeds*!"

"Hence the name of the contest," I say.

"How are you not excited about this? *Pop Idol* is on tonight. Come over and we'll watch it together and enter."

I shake my head. "I hate TV talent shows."

"It's not about the show, it's about Kyler Leeds!" Amalita

insists. Then her expression changes, and she looks me up and down.

"What?" I ask. "Is there something wrong with my clothes?"

"*Entiendo,*" she says. "You're not a real Kyler Leeds fan."

Now she's gone too far. "That's insane," I say. "I'm a *huge* Kyler Leeds fan. Last year I made my mom drive me four hours to get tickets to one of his shows because the Baltimore one was sold out."

"You'll do that and you won't watch a stupid TV show?"

"There's no point," I say. "The entire universe will enter that contest." I see J.J. coming back from his locker, Jack at his side. "Logical Man," I call to him, "what exactly are the chances that either Amalita or I would win a random drawing to meet Kyler Leeds?"

"Seriously?" Jack laughs. "Is this the Night of Dreams thing? My sister was freaking out about that this morning. She's *twelve,*" he adds pointedly.

"Kyler appeals to women of all ages," Amalita says, a dreamy expression coming over her face. "Twelve, twenty . . . anyone with good taste."

J.J. looks unimpressed. "Well, that's why the odds are not in your favor. Every girl in America's going to be entering this thing. You've got, like, a none-in-a-zillion chance."

"None in a zillion," I repeat to Amalita. "Not worth bothering."

Sean's already at a desk when I get to homeroom. He

catches my eye and smiles, but I end up in a seat in the front row, so I don't know if he looks my way during the period, and he's out the door before me. I don't expect to see him in the hall, but he's there with Reenzie and Zach. Reenzie's babbling about something, but when Sean sees me he cuts her off and falls into step next to me.

Reenzie's nostrils flare like a bull's as she witnesses this. It's not an attractive look for her, but given the cause, I very much hope I get to see it more often.

"So I feel bad I had to un-ask you to hang out yesterday," Sean says as we move down the hall.

"Un-ask?"

"Dis-ask?" he suggests.

"Un-ask's good," I say. "And it's okay. Extenuating circumstances."

"Very. How about this afternoon? Would you be up for watching practice again and then . . ." He trails off.

"Sure," I say. "That'd be great."

"Cool."

We've already walked past his next class, so he turns and heads back the other way.

"Oh, wait," he says.

I turn around and he digs in his pocket. "Here."

He hands me a quarter. I don't get it.

"Now when I see you I can ask for my quarter back. Did I mention I play quarterback?" He smiles in a knowing way that makes me melt inside, then heads down to class.

I squeeze the quarter and grin. One afternoon together and Sean and I already have an inside joke.

I'm in the middle of French class conjugating verbs in the pluperfect tense when I realize something. Sean and I have an in-joke not because we had ADAPT together, but because we hung out *after* ADAPT. We were both scheduled for ADAPT long before I wished for time alone with him, but the hang-out happened *after* the wish. Or to use the pluperfect tense, I *had wished* to hang out with Sean when he asked me to come with him on a walk.

Of course, that doesn't prove anything, really. Maybe he would have hung out with me either way.

Or maybe not.

What's for sure is I will lose my mind if I keep going back and forth. I need to test the journal. I excuse myself to the bathroom—*en français, bien sûr*—and bring my bag. I lock myself in a stall.

Bad idea. In theory, great for privacy; in practice, disgusting. I leave the stall and the bathroom and opt for a corner in the hallway. I only need a couple of minutes. Ideally no one will come out and bust me. I pull the journal out of my bag and almost scrawl down the wish, but I remember all my other wish entries started with a note to my dad.

Maybe the journal's into that.

Dear Dad, I write,

It's possible I'm insane, but it's also possible you gave me a diary that makes wishes come true . . .

which sounds even more insane now that I put it down on paper. I'd really like to know for sure, so I'm going to try something and let you know how much I wish the Tube would serve pizza instead of tamales today.

I take a second to congratulate myself on my genius. I know the lunch menu for the week. Today is tamales. They're set. There's absolutely no reason for that to change, aside from some supernatural interference.

I go back to class and somehow manage to survive through the next two torturously slow periods. The second I can, I race to the Tube as if the food weren't as likely to give me dysentery as it is to fill my stomach. I force myself to not look ahead in line. I know it makes no sense; the food either is or isn't tamales, but I feel as if peeking would jinx the result. Like the wished-for pizza would morph back into Mexican food the second before it entered my line of sight.

I even close my eyes as the lunch lady plops it onto my tray.

"Are you saying grace or praying it doesn't kill you?"

It's Sofia Brooks. I don't know her, but I recognize her from algebra. I toss her a smile then look down at my tray.

Pizza.

There's a slice of pizza on my tray.

"Excuse me," I say, feeling my pulse quicken. "Isn't it tamale day?"

"It was, but the tamales were rotten," the lunch lady says, "so we swapped out with pizza. Got a problem with that?"

I'm so giddy I almost laugh out loud. "Are you kidding? You've made my wish come true." I scooch my tray to the drinks station and gaze down at the miraculous plate of food. "I made you," I whisper to it. "You wouldn't even be here if it wasn't for me."

"What is wrong with you?" Sofia asks.

"Huh? Oh, nothing," I say, blushing as red as my hair.

"Oh, there's something," she says, and adds as she brushes past me, "Freak."

Okay, that sucked, but still, I have wished pizza into life. I'm a culinary Dr. Frankenstein. The world is my oyster-morphed-into-crab-cakes.

Unless it's just coincidence. Given the quality of Aventura High's tamales, it's not hard to imagine them showing up rotten.

Maybe the journal only works for things that were going to happen anyway . . . which means it doesn't "work" at all. Or only for things that *could* happen, which is a better explanation for Reenzie's dung-dive.

"If you could wish for anything and have it happen," I ask J.J., Jack, and Amalita when we're all settled and eating—moment to bask in the triumph—pizza, "what would it be?"

"I'd have Reenzie Tresca drop Taylor Danport flat on her ass, leaving her alone, friendless, and weeping into the

Hello Kitty pillow she secretly sleeps with every night," Amalita says, glaring across the lawn.

I follow her gaze and see Taylor laughing with Reenzie, Sean, Zach, and a bunch of other people I don't know. Taylor leans against Zach, and he has a beefy arm slung around her. I guess they're together now.

"Would you really?" I ask. "Like, for real. If you had the power and could make anything happen by wishing it, would you wish for her to get hurt?"

"Absolutamente!" she says. Then she thinks about it a second. "I don't know. Maybe not. Maybe I'd just have her old nose grow back for a day and watch her freak."

"What about you, Jack?" I ask. "What would you wish for?"

"A night with Rogue and Wonder Woman?" Jack suggests.

"Promise me you'll never write fan fiction," I say. "J.J.?"

He kind of hangs his head. "I dunno," he says, looking suddenly uncomfortable.

"Oh, come on," I say, trying to catch his eye. "I want to know."

"Yeah, you do," Jack agrees.

"Dude, seriously?" J.J. says. Then he turns to me. "I don't have a wish. I've got everything I want."

"Except a certain lady love on your arm for the Winter Formal," Jack says.

The Winter Formal's at the end of the month. Signs just started appearing in the halls this week. I honestly haven't thought about it until this second. I'm surprised it's on J.J.'s radar. I wouldn't have thought it was his deal.

"Really?" I ask. "Who?"

"Doesn't matter," J.J. says. "But yeah, okay. If I could wish for anything and make it come true, I wouldn't go revenge or comic-book fantasy. I'd go hopeless romantic."

It's funny—I don't generally think of J.J. as a romantic, but when he says that, I do. I notice the way his pale skin makes his dark eyes stand out and seem deeper and richer, like they could be full of secrets. I bet when he turns them on someone he really likes, it's intense. Makes me wonder what he was like with his ex-girlfriend Carrie Amernick.

It also makes me think about what I should do next with the journal. I don't have the chance to write in it again until I'm back on the sidelines, watching Sean's track practice.

Dear Dad, I write,

I'm going to take J.J.'s advice for my next wish. I wish Sean would ask me to the Winter Formal.

10

"So tell me, Dan Marino," I say, "when you say football's your thing, do you mean it's your Thing?"

"First of all, *not* Dan Marino, Peyton Manning. Second of all, I have no idea what you're asking me."

Sean and I have been together for a couple of hours already, which sounds obscenely long, but we spent most of that time doing homework. Correction: Sean did his homework. I've attempted to focus on *Hamlet* while stressing about whether or not my latest journal wish will come true. I listened to and read the same scene six times without taking in a word of it. Then Sean offered to help. Turns out he actually enjoys Shakespeare. He explained the scene, then helped me finish the rest of my work so we could get food.

"It is my experience," I clarify between forkfuls of fried rice, "that most people have a single all-consuming Thing they love more than anything else. Is that what football is for you, or is it just something you like to do?"

He thinks a minute. "Can it be a temporary Thing?"

"Depends," I say. "Define."

"Football's my Thing *now*. It'll probably be my Thing through college. I'd love to go pro and have it be my Thing for life, but I don't think I'm that good. So at some point I'll have to get a new Thing."

"Isn't that kind of depressing?"

"Nah," he says. "I like it. I feel like I have a pretty clear road map that goes all the way through the next six years, but then anything can happen. It's like there's all huge surprises just waiting for me, you know?"

"Huge surprises aren't always good," I say.

"That's true. But sometimes they are."

He says it with a knowing smile that makes me shiver. I'm pretty sure he means me, but I will be mortified if I say something similar back and I'm wrong. I take a drink of water to stall.

"Are you going to the Winter Formal?" he asks.

Only a miracle keeps me from choking.

"You mean do I have a date?" I ask. "No."

"Do you want to go with me?" he asks.

This time I do choke . . . but only a little. When I recover, I smile and say, "I'd love that."

He drives me home in an SUV he says was once his parents', then went through each of his three older brothers before he inherited it. The outside still looks nice, but the interior is more duct tape than leather, and the air conditioner only gasps out short bursts of air that make it feel like it's laughing at us.

Doesn't bother me. Also doesn't bother me that there's no attempted kiss when I get out of the car. I certainly wasn't expecting one, nor did I wish for one . . . though next time perhaps I should.

Inside, I say a very brief hello to Mom and Erick, then race upstairs and shut my door. I fire off a warning text first:

I am about to call you and you MUST ANSWER!!!!

Ten minutes later I've told Jenna everything.

"Are you insane?" is her response.

"I know the journal thing sounds crazy, but—"

"I'm not talking about the journal granting wishes," Jenna says. "I get that. You explained it. It's real."

This is one of the many things I love about Jenna. Anyone else would cart me away after hearing what I've said. Jenna takes it in stride. If I believe it, it's real.

"My problem," she continues, "is you wished for Sean to ask you out."

"You're serious? You've seen the pictures I texted you."

"He's hot. Doesn't matter. He likes you anyway. He might have asked you without the wish."

I frown at her through the phone. "So now you're saying the journal *doesn't* grant wishes."

94

"No! I'm saying it *does*!" I can hear the frustration in Jenna's voice. I have no clue what she's getting at, but it's obviously important. "Haven't you read 'The Monkey's Paw'?"

"Have I read the monkey's paw? Now you're just speaking in code."

" 'The Monkey's Paw.' Famous short story. A guy gets a monkey's paw that can grant three wishes."

"A cut-off monkey's paw?" I ask. "Who's going to even touch that?"

"Just listen," Jenna says. I can hear her tapping her fingers on the counter. "For the first wish the guy asks for money. How does the paw answer? His son's killed, and insurance pays off exactly the amount of money he asked for. Then he wishes his son back to life, but he shows up mutilated and decomposed. Third wish? He has to use it to send his son back to the grave."

My frown deepens. "Okay, well, I already wished for my dad to come back and he did *not* show up mutilated and decomposed. But thanks so much for putting that image in my head."

"I'm sorry," Jenna says. "My point is that in every story, wishes lead to bad consequences. Always."

"But my dad wanted me to use the journal," I say in a small voice. "He gave it to me."

"Through Eddy," Jenna reminds me. "You need to talk to her."

I'm not convinced. "Why exactly would I do that to myself?"

"There are rules to these things. Eddy might know what they are."

"'Rules to these things'?" I repeat dubiously. "How many magical wish-granting journals have you dealt with lately?"

"How many books have you read lately?" Jenna retorts.

She has me there. Jenna reads everything, and always has. At any given moment she's in the middle of an audiobook for long runs, one ebook on her phone, and one on her e-reader. All this in addition to whatever she has to read for school.

"Okay, so maybe there's rules," I cede. "But Eddy won't know them. Last time I saw Eddy she was getting ready for a hot date with my very-long-dead grandfather."

"She was sane enough to tell you about the journal," Jenna reminds me.

"Barely. And she didn't do well with direct questions. I just don't think she'd help." Plus, I have no desire to go back to Century Acres. Mom hasn't bugged me, so I figure I might be able to stay away until we all go to visit on Mother's Day.

"Fine," Jenna says. "But here's the thing. If the journal really is from your dad—and if Eddy's as crazy as you say—he wouldn't want you to use it randomly. If you ask me, you shouldn't use the journal at all. Hide it somewhere. Keep it in your bookshelf if it reminds you of your dad. Don't write in it."

There's an edge in her voice I've never heard. "You're

really freaked out about this," I say slowly. Maybe Jenna is right. Maybe I should forget about it for a while.

"There are reasons things happen the way they do," she says. "Horrible reasons, maybe, because there's no possible good one for what happened to your dad, but still, reasons. I really feel like it's dangerous to mess with that."

"So, like, have you been going to church all of a sudden?"

"Autumn, I'm serious. I'm worried about you."

"I know you are. Thank you. And I promise I'll be careful."

After we hang up, I think about what she said, then open the journal.

Dear Dad, I write.

I just can't believe you'd send me a journal that would backfire in my face when I wished on it. I get what Jenna's saying, but the only two things Eddy ever said to me that feel completely sane are that the journal is from you, and that you'd want me to write in it. So I wish Jenna would calm down and not worry about it so much.

My phone chirps while I'm writing, but I don't check it until I'm done. It's a text from Sean with a link.

I click it and end up on some sports reporter's blog post about all the reasons Peyton Manning is a better quarterback than Dan Marino.

I don't even read it before I text back.

AUTUMN: Confession, I know nothing about
    Peyton Manning, Dan Marino, or football. My
    dad liked it. He loved the Dolphins and Dan
    Marino. That's all I got.

SEAN: So I'm the one who gets to make you love
    the game?

AUTUMN: Not gonna happen. Better men than
    you have tried.

SEAN: I highly doubt that.

AUTUMN: QB = QuiteBashful?

SEAN: Quite.

I go to bed all giddy. When I wake up there's a text from
Jenna.

Sorry if I freaked

it says.

Probably worried for nothing. Just keep me
posted.

I will, I think. I'm honestly not sure how I lived without
this journal. I consider placing an order for a fire drill to
get me out of English, but I decide Jenna does have a point.
Or she did before I changed her mind. There could be rules
to the journal, and I have no idea what they are. It's pos-

sible it has a limited number of wishes in it, or maybe I can only make so many every day or every week. I should save its power for truly important things.

But as long as I have it at the ready, I am unstoppable. I can avoid any obstacle tossed in my path. I'm so excited I practically float to school.

"Isn't it a great day?" I tell J.J. when I see him at our corner.

He looks unenthused. "It's the middle of winter, it's eighty degrees, and I've been outside for all of five minutes and my shirt is stuck to my body."

"Which is a very sexy look," I say. "I'd run with it."

"If I were a lesser friend, I'd ask what you were on," J.J. says. "And if I were an even lesser friend, I'd ask you to get me some."

I almost tell him. After all, he's the one who said he'd go "hopeless romantic" with his wish, and that's what inspired me to set up the Sean date. I bet he'd be thrilled it actually worked out.

Then I remember he told me he's a debunker. He wouldn't believe the journal had anything to do with the date. Or if he did, he'd want me to use it to cast a little romance his way, and I've already decided to be thrifty with the wishes.

"Can't I just be happy to see you?" I ask as we cross the street.

"Permission granted."

I wonder how things will be with Sean today. Will he wait for me before homeroom so we can sit together? Will he meet me at my locker?

"Got a question for you," J.J. says.

I glance over at him. I expect him to be grinning, but he's looking at the ground and his hands are in his pockets.

"Everything okay?" I ask, feeling a flutter of concern.

"Oh yeah! Yeah. I just . . . I was wondering." Now he looks at me, but there's something strange in his eyes. He takes his hands out of his pockets and then shoves them back in. "This is crazy." He lets out a nervous laugh. "I mean, uh, you'd think I'd never done this before."

Now I'm staring at him. "Done what?"

"This is stupid. I'm just going to come out and say it. Autumn, will you be my date to the Winter Formal?"

I keep walking, but inside I freeze.

I did *not* expect this. At all.

But I should have, I realize. Yesterday, when Jack said J.J. wanted to ask someone, and J.J. wouldn't say who, *I* was the who. When he said he'd go hopeless romantic . . . he was thinking about me.

I can't believe this. And I've obviously waited way too long to answer. J.J.'s face goes red.

"Sorry," he says, staring straight ahead. "I shouldn't have asked."

"No, you should have," I say, then cringe at the hope in his eyes. "I mean, I totally would have said yes . . . but I already told Sean Geary I'd go with him."

"Sean Geary asked you?"

"Just last night. Sorry."

"Don't be. It's all good." J.J. runs a hand through his hair and clears his throat. "So, uh, did Jack tell you his parents are taking him and his sister to L.A. over spring break? Disneyland. We're a one-hour flight from Disney World, and they want to go to Disneyland."

I want to call him on the blatant—and ferociously lame—subject change, but what are we going to do instead, talk about how long he's felt this way? Why I've never even thought about him as more than a friend?

I'm thinking about it *now,* of course, since he put the idea in my head. J.J. would be an amazing boyfriend. He's cute. And funny. And I've loved being with him from the second we met.

But Sean makes me sweat, and not just because Florida is the stickiest state in the union (which I believe should be the new motto on their license plates). So instead of forcing the conversation back to something meaningful, I keep up my end of the Disneyland versus Disney World blather until we get to school.

Amalita and Jack are both waiting for us when we get in.

"Hey, guys!" Amalita says, and my stomach sinks at her expectant, all-knowing expression. She links her arms through both of ours and walks us toward the lockers. "How was your walk? Anything new?"

I shoot my eyes toward J.J. and see him shake his head

subtly but firmly at Amalita before he smiles. "Actually, yeah," he says. "Autumn told me she's going to the Winter Formal with Sean Geary."

"Oooh, ouch," Jack winces.

"Dude . . . ," J.J. warns. He breaks away from Amalita and pulls Jack with him toward his own locker. Amalita crosses her arms.

"What?" I finally say.

"Sean Geary?"

"I know you're not crazy about him. Trust me, there's more to him than you think."

She looks down at an imaginary chip on her green-polished nails. "Not impressed."

"Are you mad because it's Sean, or because it's not J.J.?" I ask her.

"You don't want to go out with J.J., *lo que sea,* that's between you and him. I just think you can do better than Sean. Haven't you ever heard the thing about judging someone by the company they keep?"

I smile beatifically. "That's why Sean asked me out. He judged me by you, J.J., and Jack. He couldn't resist."

"Don't make me smack you."

She doesn't smack me. We join back up with Jack and J.J. and everything seems normal again. Sean doesn't wait for me so we can sit together in homeroom, but he does wait for me afterward, and while we walk together the short distance to his next class, I promise him I'll come watch his track practice again.

Part of me wonders if disappointing J.J. was my monkey's-paw punishment for wishing Sean would take me to the dance. If it is, it's a bummer, but it's not awful. I would expect any hideous consequence to come from Reenzie, but all I get from her are dagger looks and flaring nostrils. Those aren't tortures, they're treats.

It's not until two weeks later that the rumors start.

11

This girl who used to sit at my lunch table back in Maryland once told me that you can boil a frog to death without him trying to escape. You just make the water cold at first, then slowly heat it up so he doesn't realize it's getting hotter until it's too late. She'd assured me that she'd never tried it herself, but . . . Jenna and I moved tables after that.

But that notion of not being able to react to things until you're in danger? That's pretty much what happens to me now. At first everything's fine. I'm going about my business, walking to classes, seeing my friends, hanging out with Sean after his track practices . . . totally normal.

Do I notice the whispers and the stares? A little, at first, but I can't even say when they start because they're subtle. And it's not like they're unexpected. I know Reenzie hates that Sean and I are getting close, so of course she's going to stare, and Taylor, Zach, and their group follow her lead, so I barely notice how they look at me. When other people look at me differently, I just assume it's out of a kind of respect. Sean's the hottest guy in school. And he's interested in me, the still-pretty-new girl. I'd look at me differently too.

It's not until the afternoon I'm approached by Shayla McConkle that I know something's up.

Shayla is gorgeous in a very earthy way, with long blond braids and a body made for the beach. She wears almost as much makeup as Amalita, and all her clothes are low-cut, skintight, and just this side of trashy. The girl leaves a trail of pheromones wherever she walks, but Amalita told me she's one of the most conservative people in the entire school.

Amalita, J.J., Jack, and I are walking across the lawn after dumping our lunch trays when Shayla steps directly in my path. She's wearing a very clingy tank top that reveals the lacy edge of her bra. I hear Jack gasp behind me. She looks at me sternly, and I wonder if I did something wrong to her even though I've never said a word to her in my life. I've never even officially met her.

"I want you to know I'm disgusted by what you did."

"Um . . . okay," I say. "Shayla, right? I'm Autumn."

"But when I think about the way you had to pay . . ." She pats my shoulder and tosses off a sympathetic gaze before she walks away.

"That was weird," I say, watching her go. "Any clue what it was about?"

"I'll ask Carrie," Amalita says. "She'll know."

"I'll ask her," J.J. says. "I have to talk to her anyway."

He walks off to find Carrie, and that's when I really start noticing the looks. They're coming from everywhere. And it's as if the very act of my walking past someone triggers their hand to shoot up to their mouth so they can lean over and whisper.

Whisper about me, clearly. But what?

Whatever it is, I'm pretty sure it has nothing to do with me going to the Winter Formal with Sean.

I'm watching track practice when Amalita calls.

"You are in public, am I right?" she asks.

"I'm watching track."

"Then you are not allowed to freak out. It will only make it worse."

"Make what worse? What did you hear?"

"J.J. heard. Carrie told him."

"Told him *what*?"

"Okay, here it is. *Someone* is spreading a rumor that you, um, got around back in Maryland. A lot. You got preg—"

"What?"

"There's more. You got pregnant, and your dad was so ashamed he ran off here, where he . . . I can't even say it."

I feel like the world has shrunk down to just me and the phone. I think I know what Amalita is going to say, but I need to hear the words to actually believe it. "It's okay. Tell me."

"It's *not* okay, but I'll tell you." She takes a deep breath, then blurts it out. "Everyone's saying he was so ashamed he came down here and committed suicide. The people back at home knew all about it, so you and your mom and your brother moved down here."

It's exactly what I thought she was going to say, but it's so bizarre I don't know how to react. "That doesn't even make any sense," I say. "My dad died in a car crash."

"Which he got into on purpose because he couldn't live with the shame."

"That's *insane*! Who in real life would react that way? No one! No one would react that way!"

"Remember what I said about being in public and not freaking out?"

It's true. I'm shouting, and everyone else watching track is staring, clucking, and shaking their heads.

I don't care. I have the phone in a death grip. "Did Carrie tell J.J. who started it?"

"You know who started it," Amalita says.

"But did she *tell* him?"

"She said she didn't know. I called her too; she told me the same thing. Everyone's heard it; no one knows who started it."

"And everyone believes it? Are they really that stupid?"

More stares and whispers. I want to smack all of them.

"I don't know if everyone believes it, but people love a story. This is a story."

I stare out at the field. Reenzie's right there, in her short shorts and tank top, laughing with the other pole-vaulters like she's the most innocent girl in the world.

"I'm going to kill her," I say.

"Autumn," Amalita warns, "listen. Don't do anything stupid."

I hang up. Sometimes I can be kind of impulsive. I react before I think. I cry and yell instead of behaving rationally.

This is one of those times. "Marina Tresca!"

The track team is huge. I'm sure it would be a lie to say *everyone* turns and stares, but everyone in my line of vision does just that. Doesn't matter. I'm only concerned with Reenzie. I stomp down the hill, right through the track lanes and onto the practice field.

Reenzie has the nerve to smile like we're best friends. "Hey, Autumn. What's up?"

I swing at her.

I don't even know I'm going to do it until I do.

There's just one problem: I've never hit anyone in my life, and it turns out I suck at it. Reenzie easily dodges my punch, which swings my body off balance. Reenzie, who apparently is quite good at fighting, does some kind of kick thing and sweeps my legs out from under me so I wheel around and smack down hard on the back of my head.

"Oh my God," I hear a girl say.

Everything's black. Then it's grainy and I hear thundering noise all around me.

"I have no idea, Coach Branley." It's Reenzie. "She ran out and punched me. I just tried to get away."

"Autumn? Are you okay?"

Sean is hovering over me, concern filling his beautiful

blue eyes. I wonder if this would be a good time to kiss him. I lift my head a little closer.

Ow. Lightning bolt through my brain. Moving bad. Kissing not on the agenda. Better to keep my head down.

"Are you serious?" It's Reenzie again. "You're worried about *her*? She *attacked* me."

The coach now leans over my other side. At least, I assume it's the coach. All I can really see is the whistle dangling a millimeter above my eye, dangerously close to whacking me in the nose. He puts a hand over my eyes, then pulls it away. Over my eyes, pulls it away.

"What's your name?" the coach asks.

"He's checking you for concussion," Sean says, reading my mind. "Making sure your pupils constrict and dilate. Happens in football all the time."

"Autumn Falls . . . ow . . ."

"You're okay," the coach says. He and Sean work together to help me to my feet. "You can walk? You're not going to fall over or anything?"

I take a couple steps. I'm woozy and my head is killing me, but I'm okay and I tell him so.

"Great. Head up to the principal's office. I'm gonna call so she'll be expecting you. Gotta report this."

"I'll take her," Sean offers.

"Nope, need you on the field. You." He gestures to some girl sitting on the hill with her friends. She's a freshman named Geena, but that's the full extent of what I know about her. "Can you get her to Dorio's office?"

"Sure."

Geena hops up and practically skips to my side. She's small, perky, and eager to be a part of the drama. Sean gives my hand a squeeze before Geena leads me back to the main building, and she spends the whole walk peppering me with questions about my storied past. I don't have the energy to make her shut up. I pretend I'm more out of it than I really am just so I can avoid talking.

Mrs. Dorio is waiting for me in her office. She's in what's apparently her favorite Dealing with Autumn position—arms folded, standing in front of her desk, leaning on its edge, glasses lowered just enough to peer over them.

"I believe one of the very first things I said to you is battery's an expellable offense," she notes.

"I didn't batter anyone," I say. "The only one who got battered was me."

"But you tried to start a fight," she says. She looks me up and down. "You don't strike me as the fighting type."

For all her drill-sergeant posturing, Mrs. Dorio has a sympathetic look in her eyes. "I'm not," I say. "Remember how I told you I knew who posted that picture of me on the student portal? The same girl spread a rumor about me. A bad one. About my dad. When I found out, I got angry."

"And you lashed out."

I nod, feeling as if I'm going to start crying. I really hope I don't.

"Then we're lucky you're a very poor fighter, or I'd have to take action. As it is, I think we can more or less call it a wash. Unless you have proof this person you think started the rumor really did?"

I shake my head but it hurts, so I just give a halfhearted shrug. Of course I don't have proof. Reenzie's smarter than that.

"I'll have to give you detention. And I'll need to talk to your mother. Do you think she'll be available to come in right now?"

I nod. Even if she's in the middle of a dog rescue, I know she'll drop everything if I call and say I need her. Not that I want to call her, but better me than Mrs. Dorio.

▼

Two hours later, I've been checked out and given the all clear by the nurse, and am sitting in the waiting area outside the office with Erick while Mom finishes up with Mrs. Dorio. I haven't said a word to Erick. He tried to talk at first, then retreated to his DS. Now he's kicking my chair as if it's just an inadvertent effect of swinging his legs.

Clunk . . . clunk . . . clunk . . .

"What?" I finally snap.

"Are you in trouble?" he asks.

"Hmmmm. Take a guess," I say sarcastically. "Do you want me to be in trouble?"

"Depends. Are you in trouble for something cool?"

I lean back against the wall. "I'm not in trouble. I mean, I shouldn't be."

"Oh."

Clunk . . . clunk . . . clunk . . .

I'm about to grab his leg, twist it, and *get* in trouble when Mom comes out of Mrs. Dorio's inner sanctum. She doesn't say anything until I'm with her in the front of the car and Erick's belted into the back. Mom makes him put on his headphones to play his games, then tunes the radio so it's all in the back speakers. I know he'll still listen, but I appreciate her effort.

"Why didn't you tell me you're being bullied?" she asks.

Ugh. Even the word is embarrassing. "I'm not being *bullied*," I say. "I'm being annoyed. Badly."

"Is it because you're new?" Mom asks. "Maybe if we make an effort to get to know people here . . . we could have a big party, invite whoever you think is causing the trouble."

"Mom, I'm not eight. You can't fix this with playdates."

She doesn't say anything for a while. When she does speak, her voice is so low I have to strain to hear it.

"So what was the rumor?" she asks. "Mrs. Dorio said she didn't know . . . but you said it was something about your father?"

"You don't want to know."

"Yes, I do."

I look out the window. "Believe me. You don't."

There's a road crew stopping traffic and we come to a halt. "We could switch schools," Mom offers, turning to me. "Maybe a private school?"

"That's crazy. I'm not going to run away over this."

"Well, we have to do something. I'm supposed to protect you, not send you someplace to get harassed every day."

"Not harassed. Annoyed."

Mom blows out a breath. "Fine. But I don't like it."

"Me neither," I admit. "But I'll take care of it. Not in a dumb way. I promise."

The foreman is holding up a SLOW sign and we start moving again. As we approach the house, I notice an SUV pulled up to the curb in front. I squeeze my eyes tightly for just a second to make sure I'm not seeing things. When I open them, it's still there.

"Mom, that's a friend of mine," I say, tilting my head toward the car. "Mind if I sit out here and talk? I promise we won't go anywhere."

Mom thinks it over as we get out. "Just for a little while. Then I want you inside. It's late, and you still have to eat and do homework."

"Okay." I wait for Mom and Erick to go inside; then I walk out to the street and open the passenger-side door of Sean's SUV. I'm guessing he's been here a while, because his seat's tipped back and he's asleep. I pull myself onto the duct-taped seat, pull the door closed behind me, and shake his arm until he startles awake.

"Oh!" he says. "Hey."

"Hey. How did you know where I live?"

"Online student directory," he says. "I just wanted to make sure you were okay."

"I'm fine," I say. I'm also amazed he's here. "Not that I'm complaining, but you could have texted."

"Yeah," he agrees. "I just was worried you might be mad at me."

"Because you knew?"

"I'd heard the rumor, yeah."

"And you didn't tell me."

He shakes his head. Maybe I should be mad at him, but he looks so pained and worried I can't.

"Why not?" I ask.

"Because it was ugly. And I didn't believe it. And I didn't want you to hear something horrible like that from me."

I believe him.

The SUV is parked between streetlights. The battery's on, so the dashboard lights glow dim. The radio plays softly. I have a feeling I could lean in close and try to kiss him, and he'd kiss me back. I can practically feel it, and it's absolutely perfect . . . but I can't do it until I ask him something, even if it kills the mood.

"Do you know who started it?"

"No idea."

"You don't think it was Reenzie?"

He jumps back a little and scrunches his eyebrows. The soft caress leaves his voice and instead he scoffs.

"Reenzie? Why?"

Because she's in love with you and hates that you seem to like me will only ruin the moment completely; plus, it'll probably kill any shot for moments in the future. He already told me Reenzie's like a sister to him. Obviously her evil side isn't on his radar.

Sean might be interested, but he's just like Mrs. Dorio. He won't believe me without proof.

"No reason, really," I say. "I was asking around. Her name came up."

"You shouldn't believe everything you hear," Sean says.

"I don't." He puts his hands on the steering wheel like he's ready to drive away. If I tried to lean over and kiss him now, I bet he'd duck and I'd end up with my forehead pushing down the horn. Instead I open the door.

"I should get going. Thanks for checking on me."

At least I get a smile. "See you tomorrow."

I watch him as he drives away.

This would all be much easier if Reenzie weren't in the picture. I wish . . .

Oh my God.

I walk across the front lawn and sit on the stoop. I pull out the journal from my canvas tote bag.

Dear Dad, I write,

Today was pretty awful. What Reenzie said about you . . . I'm guessing you can't hear stuff like that where you are or you'd make sure she got struck by lightning. NOT that I'm wishing for that. I'm NOT.

I read over that section twice to make sure I didn't mess up any letters and actually wish for her to be hit by a bolt from the sky. I did not.

I do have a wish, though. I wish Reenzie would get over Sean and stop doing evil things to me. I feel like this one's not much to ask, and it would make everything a million times better for all of us, even her.

I shut the journal and smile, completely satisfied.

How did I not think of this before?

Now everything will be simple.

Finally.

12

As I enter Ms. Knowles's classroom the next morning, Reenzie waves, smiles, and pats the chair next to her. I turn to see who's behind me.

"Autumn," Reenzie says, and does the whole show again. Sean's on Reenzie's other side. He's smiling too.

Subtly, so they won't see, I wipe my hand over the seat. No tacks, no glue, no ketchup. Okay, then.

When the bell rings, Reenzie gets up, smiles wide, chirps, "Bye, Autumn! See you at track practice!" and zips out of the room before I can even stand up.

That can't possibly be from the journal. The journal grants wishes; it doesn't brainwash people.

"I talked to Reenzie on the way in to school," Sean says as we walk down the hall.

I'm dying to ask if they stopped off for a quick brain transplant, but I'm kind of walking on eggshells. "Oh, yeah? What did you say to her?" I ask instead.

"I asked her to be nice to you."

"You did?"

"Yeah. But not because I think she had anything to do with starting that rumor. I don't."

I look at him. "Then why bother?"

He smiles and the corners of his mouth twitch and it's hard to stay on my feet. "I like you. So I want her to like you too. See you later, Autumn."

He lopes off to class.

Sean likes me. The fear slips off me and I relax. The Reenzie thing's more complicated, but I have faith in the journal. Maybe the forced-by-Sean nice-itude is simply the first step to her getting over him and giving up her evil ways.

Now if I can just avoid monkey's-paw backlash, everything will be fine.

I watch my back for the next few days, but it looks as though the journal really did do its job. Reenzie isn't as sickly sweet to me after that first day, but she does something even better: she ignores me. She doesn't stare, sneer, or laugh. It's not even like she goes out of her way to turn up her nose and snub me. If she happens to meet my eye, I get the same bland nothing she might give a freshman.

It's like I don't even exist.

It's a little slice of paradise.

Then I see something on the way into school one morning that's so shocking, I grab J.J.'s arm hard enough to leave a bruise.

"Do you see that?" I hiss.

J.J. doesn't answer. When I turn to face him I realize it's because he's catatonic. His mouth is wide open, and even though I watch him for a full minute, he doesn't blink once.

I turn back to the show. A red Mustang convertible sits in the back of the school parking lot, under some palm trees. The spot is shaded and well tucked away from the front entrance but very much in view of our walking route. The car's top is down, and Reenzie and a hot junior guy I recognize from track—Trevor, a sprinter—are in the backseat, making out so frantically and breathlessly it's impossible not to stare.

▼

"If she's with Trevor, I'm off her list, right?" I ask Amalita, filling her in when we get to school.

Amalita has a math quiz, and she's in deep prep mode. "Um, right. Looking good. For now." Then she goes back to her notebook.

I can't blame Amalita for being cautious. She doesn't know about the journal. Jenna does, so I text her the minute I get the chance.

Wow!

she texts back.

Journal = SERIOUS wish power. Just be careful,
OK?

I'm honestly not worried. The Winter Formal is only a
few days away now, and there are a million things I need
to do to get ready. Mom wanted to take me dress shopping,
but I told her I wanted to go with Amalita, and she seemed
okay with that. We do look at some magazines together,
though, and she loves that. I like it too. It's fun to see Mom
get so excited, even though her choices are kind of boring.

When Amalita and I hit the mall after school, we go
straight to the department stores. She finds a clingy purple floor-length gown with rhinestones up one side and
a slit to mid-thigh that would look laughable on me, but
she has the curves and personality to pull it off. When she
bursts out of the dressing room in it, she reaches her arms
out in both directions.

"How do I look?" she asks. "And how will I look with a
man on each arm?"

"Fabulous and extra fabulous," I say. Amalita, Jack, and
J.J. are going to the formal together as friends.

"You sure J.J.'s not mad at me?" I ask once she's back in
her regular clothes and we're scanning the racks.

"For saying yes to another guy before he even asked
you?" Amalita asks. "He has a crush on you; he's not insane."

She pulls out a sleeveless emerald-green dress and
holds it against me, then frowns and puts it back.

"Besides," she says, "we went as friends last year and it was really fun. Me, Jack, J.J., and Taylor. Rented a limo, went to Denny's at midnight. . . . We swore we'd do it that way every year. Which reminds me."

She scrolls through her phone, then shows me the screen. It's the four of them posed on a limousine in a parking lot. Amalita and Taylor are back-to-back on the hood of the car, Jack is dangling upside down off the roof, and J.J. is popping out of the sunroof, arms spread wide. The yellow Denny's sign shines in the background.

"Looks like fun," I say truthfully.

"I'm texting it to Taylor," Amalita says. "I'm sending her one every day this week so she'll remember what she's missing." She glances down at her phone. "Look, I know that if Taylor dumped me she's not worthy of me, but I can't stop myself from wanting to humiliate her."

I study her face. "Are you sure you want to do that?" It seems a little desperate.

Amalita nods. "She misses me. Someday soon she'll come crawling back, I'll say yes, and I'll let her hang out just long enough for her to get attached before I dump her just like she dumped me. Oooh," she says as she pulls out a dress. "This is the one. Try it on."

The dress is bright red, which I'd never pick out for myself, because with my hair I figure I'd look like an erupting volcano. It's strapless, tight on top, with a flurry of tulle that stops just above the knee.

I don't flatter myself much, but this dress looks amazing

on me. I snap a picture and text it to Jenna. I laugh out loud when I get her response.

Buy that IMMEDIATELY!!!!

"Amalita, you are a fashion genius," I say as I open the dressing room door.

"This is not something you have to tell me," she says. She walks around me, appraising the fit from all sides. "*Perfecto*," she declares. "You look so good you can even wear it on our Night of Dreams with Kyler Leeds. Assuming I invite you to join me."

"Assuming you win. Which you won't."

"Which I *will*. This is the last week of the contest. Still plenty of time for you to change your mind and enter. *If* the servers don't crash. They're expecting so many entries they think they might."

"And that's supposed to make me want to enter?" I ask.

"Someone has to win, Autumn."

"Yes," I agree. "Someone who is not me." I spin in front of the mirror. "You really think I look good in this?"

"Seriously? Amazing."

▼

Finally the day of the Winter Formal arrives. I'm in my room waiting for Sean to pick me up, and I have Jenna on Skype so she can check out the outfit, complete with

Amalita-approved heels, earrings, bracelet, hair, nails, and makeup.

"Tell me the truth. I look good?" I ask as I spin around.

"You are amazeballs gorgeous," she says. "Take lots of pictures!"

The doorbell rings.

I gasp. "Noooooo! I wanted to be down there before—"

"Well, hello! You must be Sean." My mom's extra-chirpy voice travels upstairs. "You look so *handsome*."

I squeeze my eyes shut.

"Go," Jenna says. "Love you."

"Love you more."

I click off the computer, slip off my shoes, and carry them so I can run down the steps.

"Autumn!" Mom says, then adds under her breath, "Erick, make sure you get her all the way down the stairs."

Yep, there's my brother, videotaping the whole uncomfortable scene.

"No, no video. We're not doing this. This is completely embarrassing. I'm so sorry," I add to Sean.

He doesn't look embarrassed at all. "It's cool," he says. "I don't mind."

Mom sighs, a long, deep sigh that cracks at the end. It hurts my heart. I know exactly what she's thinking, and if I look at her I'll think it too, and I don't want to. Not now.

But I look at her. She's smiling, trying hard not to cry. I take her hands.

"Mom, it's okay."

"You're so beautiful," she says, touching my cheek. "If your father could see you . . ."

Oh no. I can feel the ball of tears in my throat, rising toward the back of my eyes. If they make it, I'm lost. I blink quickly.

"Stop. Please. It's just a dance. I love you so much, but I don't want to cry."

"Of course not," she says. She takes a deep breath and smiles. "Have a fantastic time. Home by midnight."

"I promise."

"Nice meeting you, Mrs. Falls," Sean says. My mom takes a few pictures of us with her phone and then we're off.

Sean holds my hand as we walk to his SUV, and I refrain from flipping the bird behind my back, where I know one-hundred-percent positively that Erick is filming us through the window.

"You okay?" Sean asks once we pull away.

"Yeah," I say, smoothing out my skirt. "Um, I'm sorry about the drama."

"Don't be. I can't even imagine . . ." He drives for a bit, then turns and smiles. "You look incredible."

"Thanks," I say, smiling back at him. "You too."

He's wearing a dark suit, a mint-green button-down, and a gray tie. It's a very good look.

The dance is at the school gym, which should be a buzzkill, but I have to admit whoever decorated it did an amazing job. Aside from the basketball court lines on the floor, it's unrecognizable—tonight it looks like a fairyland, with small twinkling lights and tables with candles and vases of white flowers. Loud music thrums through the room, and Sean and I quickly meld into the crowd of dancers. The dim light and formal clothes make it almost impossible to recognize some of these people, but Taylor's there with Zach, and Reenzie with Trevor. They don't bother me. I'm dancing with Sean, his eyes are locked on mine . . . it's perfect.

At one point, the DJ puts on a song I don't know. Sean, however, lights up.

"Do you swing dance?" he shouts over the music.

"Swing dance?" I repeat incredulously.

I have never known anyone who swing dances, but I realize that even though a lot of people have cleared off the dance floor, the ones who remain swirl in holding-hand couples, jumping and twirling and gliding together in a way I've only seen in the movies.

"It was a thing when we were kids," Sean admits. "A bunch of us took lessons. Hated it then, but it's actually pretty fun. Want to try?"

He holds out his hand. His smile is enticing. So is the idea of him whirling me around on the dance floor.

"You do realize I'm the least coordinated human being on the planet," I say over the music.

"Just let me lead you," he says.

I give him my hand.

In the movie version of my life, the next four minutes

would be an exhilarating whirlwind. We'd move as a single unit around and around the floor, and end the song with him balancing me in a gravity-defying dip.

In reality . . .

"Ow! Oh God, I'm sorry. . . . Wait. . . . Oh no . . . shoot . . . ow!"

I can't go two steps without tromping on his toes, making him step on mine, or smacking heads. No matter how many times he tells me to let go and just follow, I can't do it. Does this say something good about my strong, independent personality? No doubt.

It also makes me a crappy dance partner.

"Forget it," he says. "We'll wait for the next song."

He's not a jerk about it or anything, but I see the way he watches the other dancers and I know he's disappointed. Then I see Reenzie. Apparently Trevor missed dance lessons when he was a kid too, because he's talking to Zach while his date looks longingly at the couples on the floor. I notice her catch Sean's eye and shrug.

"You should dance with her," I tell him impulsively.

Sean looks surprised. "Really? You don't mind?"

Shockingly, I don't. He's here with me, Reenzie's here with Trevor, he wanted to dance with me first . . . it's cool.

"Thanks." He walks over to Reenzie and says something into her ear and reaches for her hand. She looks to Trevor as if asking his permission, but he's not even paying attention. She shrugs again, takes Sean's hand, and a second later they've turned from high school sophomores to professional dancers, bopping across the floor as though they're in *Dancing with the Stars.*

Unlike me, Reenzie follows Sean flawlessly. With the exception of those moments he spins her away, their eyes stay locked, and it's like they're reading each other's minds. I find it hard to believe they haven't spent the last ten years rehearsing this moment.

They look disturbingly happy.

I remind myself this was my idea. I told him to dance with her.

That doesn't mean I have to watch it.

I head to the refreshments table. Jack is there downing punch while Amalita nibbles a cookie.

"Hey, Autumn," Jack says, wiping his mouth on his jacket sleeve.

Amalita looks at me closely. "Are you okay with them out there?"

I nod. "Totally. And the song's almost over. Where's J.J.?"

Amalita tilts her head toward the dance floor. J.J.'s swing dancing with a pretty girl with bobbed brown hair. She wears a fringed dress, beads, and a shimmering headband. She looks adorably as if she stepped out of a time machine from the 1920s.

"Is that . . . Carrie Amernick?" I ask, recognizing her.

"Yes," Jack grumbles.

"Carrie's J.J.'s date?" I ask. "I thought he came with you guys."

"She asked him at the last minute," Amalita explains.

"Like . . . a date?" I ask, surprised. "They're together now?"

"Emergency date," Jack grouses. "Hers got the flu. And did she call *me*, the guy who'd love to go out with her, or did she call *him*, the guy who broke up with her last year?"

"He broke up with *her*?" I ask. For the first time I imagine J.J. as boyfriend material. "What were they like together?"

"Listen to you," Amalita says. "What are you, jealous?"

"No," I scoff as I help myself to a cup of punch.

I'm *not* jealous. I'm interested. Carrie swing dances like me . . . which is to say, like an elephant in a three-legged race. J.J. isn't bothered, though. He moves very slowly, far off the beat, so he can teach her each step. It never works, but he doesn't get frustrated. Every time she messes up, they both laugh. When the song ends, she falls into his arms and they hug.

Not romantically. It's a friendly hug. Maybe she'd like it to be romantic, but he broke up with her last year. He's in friend mode.

A slow song starts up, and I figure J.J. and Carrie will join us at the refreshments table. I adjust my dress. J.J. hasn't seen it yet, and I think he'll like it. Maybe he'll make an anagram about how it looks on me. I should come up with one about him in a suit. He looks good. I mean, he doesn't have the body to fill out a suit the way Sean does, but . . . still nice.

Instead of joining us at the table, J.J. and Carrie stay

in their hug. He slides his arms down to her waist and she curves hers around his neck.

I don't even think he knows I'm here with Jack and Amalita. His eyes don't leave Carrie's until she pushes herself into his personal space and rests her head on his chest. Then he closes his eyes.

"Autumn, wake up," Amalita says as Sean walks up to me.

"Hey. Did you watch?" he asks, his hair tousled. He loosens his tie a little.

"Yeah!" I say, blinking back into the moment. "You guys were great."

"Way too many hours performing in the basement for parents who wanted to make sure they got their money's worth."

I smile at him. "Looked like you guys had a lot of fun."

"We did. But I'd have a lot more fun dancing with you."

He holds out his hand. My stomach flutter-flips as he leads me out to the dance floor. He wraps his arms around my waist. Before I rest mine over his shoulders I make the move I've wanted to do since I first saw him. I run my hands down Sean's arms. Unbelievable. Even through the sport coat I can feel his muscles.

"Is there something on my sleeves?" Sean asks.

"Yeah," I say. "A little fuzz. It's gone now."

"Thanks."

We sway to the music. This time I have no problem following Sean's lead. Limited range of motion. That's the key.

"I'm really glad you're here with me," Sean says quietly.

"Me too," I whisper.

He stares into my eyes. I stop breathing.

And then his lips touch mine, and everything else in the world collapses into that kiss.

13

"You look happy," J.J. says when I meet him at our corner on Monday.

"That's because I had an amazing weekend," I say, rocking back on my flip-flops.

"Good time at the Winter Formal?"

I nod. "Fantastic. Sorry we didn't really get to hang out."

"No worries," he says. "You looked great."

"Thanks. I didn't know you saw anyone but Carrie Amernick. Or should I say, 'A Crankier Crime'?"

J.J. grins. "You looked up an anagram for Carrie's name?"

"How do you know I looked it up?" I say. "How do you know I didn't just come up with it right now?"

"'J.J. Austin Rocks a Bow Tie.' Go."

I try to picture the letters in my head. They jump around in weird combinations that may or may not be words. "I need more than a *second*," I say. "But you did rock the bow tie," I admit. "It looked particularly good at Denny's."

"Ames sent you the pictures?"

I nod again. "So what about you and Carrie? Are you guys together now?"

He kicks a plastic water bottle someone tossed on the sidewalk, sending it flying. "I don't know. She wants to be. We'll see. How about you and Sean?"

I shrug. "Not sure. He invited me to hang out with him at his house yesterday, which was great, but all we did was watch football."

"Which games?"

"Football games."

J.J. laughs. "Sounds like you had a great time."

I take a deep breath, not sure if I want to jump into this with him. "Is it weird that he didn't kiss me?"

"He did kiss you."

I can feel my cheeks turning pink. "You saw that?"

"You clearly underestimate my powers of observation," J.J. says, waggling his eyebrows.

"He did kiss me," I say slowly, "but just that night. Not yesterday. I feel like that's weird."

"Not necessarily," J.J. says. "I mean, if it were me, once that bottle was uncorked I'd want to keep drinking it. But that's just me. His head could be anywhere."

"I'm letting the bottle-corking-drinking thing go because I appreciate your advice, but seriously, it's kind of gross."

"Noted," J.J. says.

We've been walking slower than usual, so by the time

132

we get to school we have to race to homeroom. It's a shame, because I wanted to see if Sean might be waiting for me at my locker. I'm hoping he at least saved me a seat in class.

Everyone stares when I walk in.

Everyone except Sean, who concentrates hard on the top of his desk.

There is no empty seat next to him. The only open seat is at the front of the room, and I feel as if I'm swimming through a thick sea of disgust to get there.

My skin tries to crawl off my body. I've felt this before. Reenzie did something. Another picture. Another rumor. It's the only explanation . . . but it's impossible. I wished on the journal for her to stop doing evil things to me. I get that "evil" can mean a lot of different things, but given the weight of everyone's stares, I'm pretty sure whatever she did qualifies.

When Ms. Knowles looks down at her attendance book, a wadded-up piece of paper flies over my shoulder and lands on my desk. I open it up. A not-so-friendly word is printed there.

I crumple it up and throw it on the ground. What did Reenzie do?

When Ms. Knowles dismisses us, several people "accidentally" slam into me on their way out the door. My books go flying. No one hangs out to help me pick them up. Not even Sean.

When I finally get into the hall, Sean isn't there, but Amalita is.

"Tell me it's not you," she says. "I mean, I *know* it's not you, just tell me it's not you."

"I don't know what you're talking about!"

"Good. Okay. But you need to know. Come on. *Vámanos.*"

She leads me to one of the study carrels on the lower floor of the library. "Ames, I have a class," I say.

"You think I don't? This is more important."

There's a computer in the carrel and she types in a URL. What loads up is an orange background with a title on one side and a paragraph of type on the other. The title reads:

THE WINTER OF MY DISCONTENT
A True Account of Life at Aventura High

"What is this?" I ask.

"Read."

It's hard because I'm stressed, and letters always jump around more when I'm stressed. I eventually have to put a finger on the screen and run it past each word as I scan it, just to keep track.

Two months ago, I moved to Aventura, Florida. In the short time since then I've been the victim of bullying, harassment, and abuse. While I've reported these crimes to the proper authorities at my school, no action was taken because I have no proof of who was behind them. With no perpetrator to name, I can only blame the school community as a whole. With no hope for justice within the system, my only recourse is to turn the tables on those who have wronged me. My goal is not to spread rumors or lies, only to shine a harsh light on other people's secrets the way they've done with mine. I remain anonymous only for my own protection, and publish this website with great sadness in my heart.

My heart is now throbbing from somewhere inside my throat. "People think this is me?"

Amalita raises an eyebrow. Of course they think it's me. It's my story exactly except twisted—no one ever shined a harsh light on any of my secrets; Reenzie made my secrets up.

"The name doesn't hurt either," Amalita says.

I look at the URL: winterofdiscontent.com.

"What, people think I like Shakespeare?" I ask. "Has no one seen me in English class?"

"You're serious?" Amalita asks. "*Winter* of discontent. You're *Autumn* Falls."

"Yeah, but that's stupid," I say.

"Stupid enough for people to interpret it as a clue that it's you. You come off as someone trying to get revenge while staying anonymous."

I let out a strangled laugh. "*I'm* not getting revenge!"

"I'm just saying," Amalita says slowly, "that's what people think. Hit the Enter Site button. It gets worse."

"Great."

I click the link and end up on another orange-background page. This one has a single column of text broken up into bullet-pointed paragraphs.

- **Sofia Brooks:** *Your family's on welfare, but you just bought a pair of $400 sandals? Let's say they were secondhand. Guarantee no less than $200. Really bad choice, or klepto? You tell me.*

- **Shayla McConkle:** *You're the reason we got the dress code memo last year about not wearing inappropriate things to school. So when are you going to lose the tight tank tops and short skirts? Besides, they're doing those thighs of yours no favors.*

- **Amalita Leibowitz:** *Don't worry, a heat rash in your stomach folds is nothing to be ashamed of. Oh wait, yes it is.*

"Oh my God," I say. "Tell me you didn't think I actually wrote this."

"No!" Amalita scoffs. She shoots me a quick glance, then looks down at the computer.

"Okay, maybe for like a second," she admits, "but I know better. Taylor's the only person who knew about that."

I stare at her, my eyes wide. "That's real?"

She nods. "Intertrigo, two years ago, we're not talking about it."

"So you think Taylor did this?" I ask.

Amalita shakes her head. "Taylor's weak, she's disloyal, and *necesita que la den una colleja*, but she wouldn't do this. Reenzie and her genius brother are the ones who put this up."

"But she was supposed to stop being evil to me," I say in a small voice.

Amalita snorts. "Says who?"

I don't answer. I keep reading "Winter's" revelations. I force myself to read slowly and carefully so I don't miss a word. Each bullet point is nastier and more personal than the last. I feel light-headed. At least Amalita's here if I pass out.

My hands feel clammy, as if I've been holding them over a pot of boiling water. "This one makes no sense. *'Reenzie Tresca: Thought you could keep your "exclusive" Sweet Sixteen party at the Firefly Club a secret? Sorry. I know all about it, and now so does everyone else.'* That's not even a dig."

"She's bragging," Amalita says. "The Firefly Club is this *muy exclusivo* event spot. Reenzie wants everyone to know she's having her party there, but this way she's not the one rubbing all our noses in it."

"Plus, she's named on the list so people won't think she wrote it," I add.

"Smart," Amalita says, sounding almost like she admires her.

"It's *devious*! Beyond devious." Who does something

like this? And how long did she plan it? "This list goes on forever!"

I'm scrolling and scrolling, looking for the end, when my eye catches on a name that makes me gasp.

◄ **Sean Geary:** *Auditory Processing Disorder? Let's just call it what it is: slightly retarded. If eight years of ADAPT hasn't gotten you off the short bus, nothing will.*

"I'm going to kill her," I say, pushing back my chair so hard a boy in the study carrel next to us picks up his stuff and moves. I think actual steam is pouring out of my ears. "No. I'm going to slowly torture her, and then I'm going to kill her."

"Works for me," Amalita says.

I rest my head in my hands and rub my temples.

"How long has it been up?" I mumble.

"From what I heard, Sunday night. I only saw it during homeroom."

I sit there for a long time. If I could will myself to disappear I would.

"Autumn?" Amalita finally says, her voice low. I can tell she's worried about me. Well, she has good reason to be.

"I have to go," I say suddenly. "I can't be here."

She doesn't try to talk me out of it. She walks me to my locker, where an envelope sticks out from between the slats.

"Mrs. Dorio?" Amalita asks.

I don't have to open it to know that's exactly who it's from, but I do anyway, and nod.

"I'll tell her you went home sick," Amalita offers.

"That's okay," I say, "I'll get it over with."

The principal's office is becoming a home away from home for me. Ironic, since I've yet to do a single thing wrong since I set foot in this school.

"Autumn, Autumn, Autumn . . . ," Mrs. Dorio sighs when I enter. She's sitting behind her desk for once instead of leaning in front of it, and turns her computer monitor so I can see the orange-background *The Winter of My Discontent* title screen.

"I realize you feel like we've failed you," she says, "but there are better ways than this to get satisfaction."

My blood boils, but my fury makes me brazen. I rest my arms on her desk and lean in so I'm the one looking down on her. I speak calmly and slowly, enunciating every word.

"Mrs. Dorio, every time I've asked you for help, you've told me you can't do anything unless you have proof. I know what this looks like, but can you *prove* it was written by me and not someone pretending to be me?"

She blinks several times. I think I actually surprised her.

"No," she says. "Not at the moment."

"Then until you can, I expect you to assume I'm innocent," I say, "or just like you suggested, I'll have my very angry parent come after you with harassment charges."

I storm out. I'm sweating and my heart is pounding, but I feel good. I plan to grab my stuff and leave before I have to face anyone else, but class ends and the halls fill with people.

Someone slams into me and sends me hurtling into the wall. I hear laughter, but I don't bother to turn to see who it was. Then someone pushes me hard from behind and I stumble into Sofia Brooks. She looks friendly until she realizes it's me.

"You're seriously going to get in my face?" she asks. "You want to talk about my shoes? Why don't you get a good look at them first?"

"Sofia, I swear, it wasn't me," I say. "I have no idea about your financial circumstances. How would I know?"

She's not listening. In fact she's pulling back her arm to throw a very sharp-heeled shoe.

I run for it, but only make a few steps before the shoe slams into my spine. "OW!"

Just have to get to my locker. I stagger forward but trip over a leg I swear wasn't stuck in my path a second ago. I smack face-first onto the floor.

Maybe I should just lie here until everyone gets into class. Or commando-crawl into a corner and curl into a ball. Instead I get up and see . . .

"Sean. Hey . . ."

He's no more than two feet in front of me, but he only flicks his eyes at mine and keeps walking.

"Are you kidding me? *Sean.*"

I grab his arm. He yanks it away, but he stops walking.

"Hey," he mutters.

"It wasn't me."

"I know," he says, but his eyes flit around as if he's worried about who will see him talking to me.

"Do you? I mean, think about it. Never mind the fact that I *wouldn't*, it makes no sense. I'm in ADAPT too. Why would I say that?"

Sean nods, but he doesn't look at me. "I've got to go," he says.

And he's gone.

"Autumn!"

I look up expecting another furious victim, but it's J.J. And he's smiling. I try to remember if the website said something horrible about him. I'm sure it did.

"Hey," I say nervously.

"You look like you could use an armed escort." He holds out his arms. "Sadly, these are the best I can do." He drapes one of them over my shoulder, a gesture that would have felt intensely out of place just two hours ago, but now I'm so grateful I could cry. People still glare at me, but they're not physically attacking.

"They hate me," I say, my bottom lip quivering. "They all hate me."

"They don't know you," he says. "They don't know how insane it is to think you'd put up a site like that."

"When did you see it?"

"Jack showed it to me in first period. He was not

pleased about the size of his manhood being maligned, but I reminded him you'd have no way of knowing. Amalita told me you're going home. Want me to walk you?"

"I'm okay. Thanks."

I want to call Jenna on the way home, but of course she's in class. Maybe I could wish for a freak blizzard to hit Maryland so she'd get out and we could talk.

Like I wished for Reenzie to stop being evil to me.

Did the journal ever work at all?

I can't figure it out. It seemed as if it did, but maybe it was pure coincidence.

The weird thing is, the more I turn it over in my head, the more I feel like it would help to get it all down on paper.

In the journal.

When I get home, no one's there but Schmidt. I scoop him up and plop down on the couch, then pull out the journal.

Dear Dad, I write. *I'm so confused.*

I tell him everything. I keep hoping for some grand epiphany, but it doesn't come. By the time I get to the part about the website, I'm feeling so furious and helpless I have to blink away tears to keep going.

What makes me so crazy is that it's insane, I write. *There's no logical reason for one person to be this vicious to anyone else. It wouldn't even make sense if I'd specifically targeted her actual boyfriend and stole him away . . . but I didn't! I didn't do anything, and I definitely didn't do anything to deserve all this. I wish*

I pause. Does it even make sense to wish on the journal anymore?

Probably not, but this is something I'd say whether or not the journal has powers, so I keep going.

I wish she could know how it feels, I write. *I wish that next time, Reenzie's the one who gets hurt.*

I spend the rest of the day watching bad TV. By the time Mom and Erick are supposed to come home, I'm exhausted. I leave a note on the kitchen table that says I came home sick, then climb upstairs and crawl right into bed. A couple times I half hear my phone ring. The rings pause, like someone got my voice mail, then start all over again. I ignore them and fall back asleep.

When I finally open my eyes, it's dark out. I flip on my night-table lamp and find a note from Mom.

Hope you feel better.
Lasagna in the fridge if you're up for it.
Love you.

My phone's ringing again. It's Amalita.

"Did you hear about the crash?" she asks breathlessly.

For a second I can't fathom what she means. Is she talking about the *Winter of My Discontent* website?

Then I remember. The Kyler Leeds contest. Tonight was the last night to enter. Amalita told me they were expecting so many entries the servers could crash. I'm both stunned and amused that with everything else going on she can still get this excited about a stupid contest on TV.

"You shouldn't sound so surprised," I say. "Didn't you tell me they pretty much knew it was going to happen?"

"What are you talking about?" she asks.

"The Kyler Leeds contest."

"*The Kyler Leeds contest?*" She says it like she's saying "*The puppy-slaughtering contest?*"

"Yeah," I say. "What else?"

"Autumn, I'm talking about Reenzie."

"What about her?"

"Her *car* crash. She's in the emergency room."

Cold washes over me like I've been dipped in a freezing lake. I can't speak.

"Autumn?" Amalita asks. "You there?"

"Yeah," I mumble. I grab the journal and flip to my last entry, even though I already know what I'll read.

I wish that next time, Reenzie's the one who gets hurt.

Oh my God . . . what did I do?

14

I press Amalita for details, but she doesn't have any, so I quickly hang up and call Sean.

He doesn't answer. No doubt he's mad at me for the website I didn't write.

Two seconds after I hang up, my phone chirps with a text.

> SEAN: Saw you called. Can't talk now.

> AUTUMN: No problem. Heard about Reenzie—
> what happened?

> SEAN: Car crash. Her brother home from school
> and driving. Fell asleep at the wheel, hit a
> phone pole. Reenzie wasn't wearing seat belt
> and thrown from car.

> AUTUMN: OMG . . . is she okay?

SEAN: Yeah. Broke her leg in three places. Could have been a lot worse.

AUTUMN: Wow . . .

SEAN: Gotta go. At ER with Reenzie's and my parents. They're letting her out soon. See you tomorrow.

AUTUMN: Definitely.

There is an ugly, shallow part of me that is incredibly happy right now. Not about Reenzie's crash. That's horrifying. I'm incredibly happy that even though Sean's at the emergency room waiting to see if his practically-a-sister will be okay, he still texted me. He obviously can't be that mad.

It's way too late, but I call Jenna. Her phone rings several times. Her parents won't be happy if they hear her ringtone, but they like me, so hopefully they'll get over it quickly.

"Is somebody dead?" Jenna grumbles sleepily.

"I wished that Reenzie would get hurt and she ended up breaking her leg in three places in a car crash," I blurt out, clutching the phone so tight my knuckles turn white.

"What?" Jenna's voice is clear now. She's awake. I tell her everything and send her to the website so she'll understand how mad I was, then read her the end of my journal entry word for word. I finish with the details from Sean.

"That's it," she says matter-of-factly. "You have to get rid of the journal."

"I was thinking the same thing." I pick up the book. I feel the soft leather and stare at the triangular face on the cover. It looks oddly sad.

"But I'm not sure I can do that," I admit. "It's part of my dad." Throwing out the journal would be like severing a connection to him.

"You don't know that, remember?" Jenna reminds me. "That's just what Eddy said."

"I know, but that's how it feels," I say, swallowing. "When I write in it, I write to him."

"Okay . . . okay . . ."

I can picture her pacing around the circular rug in her room, as if it's a mini running track.

"You need to go see Eddy," she finally says. "I know we've talked about it before, and I know she's nuts, but this is serious now. You have to find out if she knows anything that can help."

I don't relish the idea of going back to Century Acres, but Jenna's right, so I reluctantly promise her I'll go tomorrow after school.

After I hang up I stare at the journal a long time before I fall asleep.

▼

"Brave woman," J.J. says as I fall into step with him the next morning.

"What do you mean?"

147

He raises an eyebrow, and I remember the *Winter of My Discontent* site. I've been so upset about the horror I did do that I haven't thought about the horror I didn't.

"Still bad?" I ask.

"By the end of the day, a few wise souls wondered how you could possibly know a lifetime's worth of dirt about people you met a couple months ago."

"Mmmm, you think?" I say sarcastically. "Thank you."

"But they were vastly outnumbered by idiots with the opposite opinion, many of whom swore they saw you spying on people and taking notes every day at track practice."

I turn to stare at him. "I wasn't taking notes, I was watching Sean!"

"Which I mentioned when I was in earshot," he says. "I don't know, maybe it'll be better today. Everyone has something else to talk about."

We're walking through the parking lot now, and we see Reenzie. She's in the passenger seat of Sean's SUV, which he pulled up to the curb. Her door is open, and she dangles sideways on the seat. Her right leg is in a purple cast that goes all the way up to the middle of her thigh.

"Seriously?" I ask. "She was in the emergency room last night. How is she at school today?"

J.J. snorts. "Are you kidding? She's in paradise. There's even a Twitter account devoted to her cast."

There's a huge crowd gathered around Sean's car. They all gape as Reenzie slowly scoots to the edge of her seat. She waits, wincing, as Sean yanks out a pair of crutches.

He brings them around to her and holds them while she eases herself out of the car and onto her good foot.

A crowd of gawkers surrounds Reenzie, pelting her with questions and looking generally amazed that she's actually standing in their presence. I watch as Sean parks his car, then walks over with his backpack as well as Reenzie's metallic-and-canvas tote bag, which, of course, he carries for her, proving that he is a gentleman. J.J. and I wait until they're all inside so we won't have to squeeze past, then head in ourselves. Jack and Amalita are right there and immediately stop me from apologizing about the website.

"We know it wasn't you," Jack says, shoving his hands in his pockets. "And if you really must know—"

"Some things are better left unsaid," Amalita cuts him off, giving me a smile that reminds me that I do have friends here. I can get through this.

It's so good and normal hanging out with my friends that I can almost forget that the rest of the school hates me. Until I walk down to homeroom and once again become a human pinball. I don't know if it's good or bad that I'm so used to the hiss of expletives I barely hear them.

Sean smiles, but no one else even looks at me. All eyes are still on Reenzie, tucked into a desk in the back, her purple-cast-covered leg thrust out to the side.

I sit across the room and surreptitiously watch her all through homeroom. She looks terrible. Beautiful, of course, but pale and glazed over. A cynical part of me wonders how much of that is for show, but even if she's playing it up, she still has to be in terrible pain.

And it's my fault. I did that to her.

When homeroom ends, Sean carries her bag while Reenzie crutches her way to the bathroom. I follow. Sean doesn't notice me until she's through the door and he's alone.

"Oh, hey." He looks as though he wants to say something but now's not a good time.

"Hey," I say. "I'll talk to you later, okay?"

I slip into the bathroom and hang by the sinks. I can see one of the stall doors is closed, and I try to imagine the mechanics of handling everything with one leg fully extended. Should I try to help?

I wait.

It takes a long time, but eventually she comes out and crutches her way over to the sinks. She wrinkles her face when she sees me. I'm sure it looks weird that I'm just standing there, stalking her in the bathroom.

"What are you doing here?" she asks.

"I just . . ." I gesture to her leg. "I'm sorry. I'm really, really sorry."

My apology is clearly not welcome. "Why? You didn't do it."

There's no good response to that, but I still feel like I should say more. I stand there while she washes her hands.

"You want to be sorry for something," she says coldly, "you should be sorry for that website. *Winter of My Discontent*? Everyone knows it's you."

"It's not me," I say, trying to stay in control. "I have an idea who did it, but I can't prove it. I will, though."

"Good luck with that."

She tries to hobble out of the room, but I plant myself in her way.

"What's your deal with me, Reenzie?" I ask her flat out. "What did I do?"

Reenzie leans on her crutches until our faces are close. "Things just work better when everyone knows their place," she says.

She lifts her left crutch and I think she's going to smack me with it, but instead she reaches it past me and bangs it against the door, smashing it open.

I watch her hobble away with Sean, then pull out my phone and text Jenna. Just spoke to Reenzie, I write. Somehow not so upset about breaking her leg anymore.

Jenna doesn't text back until lunch. Break well deserved but journal still rogue nuke. Talk to Eddy.

She's right. Century Acres also has the benefit of being one place I won't run into anyone trashed on "my" website. I take the bus there right after school. There's no piano player in the lobby today, so I ask at the front desk if Eddy's in her room.

"Honey, it's four o'clock," the attendant says. "She's having dinner. The dining room's down the hall and to the left."

"Thanks."

In the dining room, Eddy's holding court. She's at a

round table with six other white-haired women, all of whom watch her, entranced. Eddy's on her feet, telling a story with her whole body, like she's using sign language. Or doing a hula. She freezes when she notices me, then spreads her arms wide.

"Autumn! My beautiful granddaughter!" She waggles her fingers until I come close enough for her to hug me tight. Then she pulls my head down and kisses me on the lips. It disturbs me that this is more action than I get from Sean.

"Pull up a chair and sit," Eddy says. "Have dessert." She lowers her voice to a stage whisper and says, "Not the chocolate ice cream, though. They put sleeping pills in it. So we don't bother the staff at night."

The women all smile politely at me and then begin talking and eating again. "Actually, can I talk to you?" I ask my grandmother. "It's kind of important."

"You need me, *querida,* I'm here for you. Let's go to my room." She winks. "These people can't keep a secret for anything."

The group at the table murmurs good-byes as Eddy hooks her arm through mine and cuddles in close as we walk. She recites a steady stream of Real Housewives of Century Acres gossip until she's settled in her favorite chair and I've closed the door to her room.

"Okay, *cariño,*" she says. "Now we talk about the journal."

"How did you know that's what I wanted to talk about?" I ask, incredulous.

"You wrote in it, *sí?*"

"*Sí*," I say.

"And something happened that maybe you didn't expect?"

There's a playful twinkle in her eyes. She doesn't get it. "Not just that I didn't expect. Eddy, I *hurt* someone."

"With the book?"

"Yes!" I say frantically. "I could have killed her. Why didn't you tell me what the journal could do?"

Eddy's hands flutter nervously in her lap. "I didn't know. I *don't* know. I only know what Reinaldo told me. Taino magic, it's not certain. I didn't want to tell you something that wasn't true."

"Don't worry about that," I say, brushing that train of thought aside. "I want to know everything."

"You have the book with you?"

I pull it out of my bag and give it to her. She smiles as she runs a hand over the cover. "This picture," she says, "you know what it is?"

"It's a face, right?"

"*Sí*, but not just a face. A three-point *zemi*. The Taino, the ancient people of Cuba, they believed the *zemi* held the spirits of ancestors, of the dead."

"This is a *zemi*?" I ask. "This picture? You think it holds dead spirits?" The idea kind of freaks me out a little bit.

"Maybe a piece of a spirit," Eddy says. "A guardian to help you through a difficult time. Some say I'm a little *chochea*." She taps her head and raises an eyebrow. "But when I hold this book, I feel closer to Reinaldo. Don't you?"

"I do," I admit. "When I write in it, it's to him."

Eddy nods. "My husband's family," she says, "the Falcianos, they descend from the *bohiques*. These are Taino healers. They know how to reach the *mundo de los espíritus,* the spirit world. This ability, over the generations, it comes and it goes. Your grandfather had none of it, but Reinaldo . . . he was a true *bohique*. He knew the spirit world, and it told him things. It whispered secrets about the fate of his loved ones, and it told him he'd be joining them sooner than he'd have liked."

"You said that before," I remind her, "that he knew he was going to die."

"You know the story, *sí?* Why he named you Autumn Falls?"

I nod. "My mom told me."

"She told you what she knows, I tell you what I know. Reinaldo told me that like that season, that bridge combining the extremes of summer and winter, his little girl would have a mission. *Un destino.* To help bring peace and harmony to the world."

"My dad told you my mission is world peace?"

Eddy laughs. It's a warm, cozy sound. "No, *querida,* not the way you're thinking of it. Your *destino* is to bring peace and harmony to your own little corner of the world. That's enough. That flows. The journal . . . well, Reinaldo hoped it would help you. And you tell me it works, *sí?*"

"Kind of," I say, thinking about everything that's happened since I've had the journal. "When I wish for something . . . when I actually use the words 'I wish,' the thing sort of happens. But a lot of it could be coincidence."

Eddy is studying me closely. "You really believe that?"

I realize I'm biting my lip hard. I stop. "No."

"Good," she says, sounding pleased. "You shouldn't. The journal brings you what you wish, but there are limits."

"Like what?" I ask, moving closer to her.

"Reinaldo told me three things it cannot do," she says. "There may be more, I don't know."

"What three things?"

"One," she says, holding up a finger, "the journal cannot change history."

"Which means it can't bring someone back from the dead," I say, not meeting her eyes.

Eddy smiles and puts her hand on my leg. "I'd have tried it too. *Immediatamente.*"

"What's the second thing?"

"Nothing impossible. The journal won't make you fly, it won't let you walk through walls."

That's probably a blessing in disguise. "Got it," I say. "And the third?"

"If it doesn't work, that doesn't mean it doesn't work."

I tilt my head. "I don't get it. If it doesn't work, how can that not mean it doesn't work?"

"The journal is like a mule. It's *obstinado.* You ask it to do something, sometimes it says no."

She yawns, wide and long.

"*Es tarde,*" she says. "You should go. Get some sleep."

It's five o'clock.

"But I still don't understand," I press, eager to learn as much as I can while she's making sense. "'Peace and harmony' is pretty vague. What exactly am I supposed to get the journal to help me do?"

She beckons me close so she can give me another kiss. "*Que pases buenas noches,* Autumn," she says. "And *no preocuparse.* You'll find the answer you need. Your father knew. This is the thing you were made to do."

And then she wants to watch the evening news and I can tell that our Q&A session is over for today.

I call Jenna while I wait for Mom to pick me up.

"She said that?" Jenna asks. "She said it's the Thing you were made to do?"

"Yeah," I say, nodding even though she can't see me. "The Thing. Bringing peace and harmony to my little corner of the world. According to Eddy—and I guess my dad—that's my Thing." I can barely believe it. I have a Thing.

"So how are you going to do it?" Jenna asks.

That's a good question. "I don't know," I admit, frowning. "I mean, right now I've got nothing even close to peace and harmony. My entire school except for Jack, J.J., and Amalita hates me."

"So you'd have to change that, right?"

"Uh, yeah."

Mom pulls up, so we click off.

"How's Eddy?" Mom asks as I climb into the car.

I'd love to tell her everything, but I know how she feels

about Eddy's supernatural ravings. Plus, I'm pretty sure the idea of Dad's soul—even part of his soul—hiding out in a journal would upset her a lot. I use a sliver of my brain to carry on a happy conversation with her and keep the rest on the journal.

What should I wish?

My life would definitely be more peaceful and harmonious if people liked me, if I were popular . . . but that's not really what I'm about. I don't need everyone to think I'm amazing. I just want them to know I'm not what Reenzie's made them believe.

That's it. When we get home I run upstairs and throw open the journal.

Dear Dad, I write, and go on to tell him all about my conversation with Eddy, and how I've been thinking about exactly the right wish.

So here's the deal, I continue writing. *Aventura High is a living land mine for me, and it's going to stay that way unless I can prove the truth. So that's what I want. I wish for justice. I wish that everyone at that school could find out exactly what Reenzie did to me, and see her for the person she really is.*

I head down to dinner completely satisfied.

Justice is on its way, and it's gunning for Reenzie Tresca.

15

Justice may indeed be on its way, but it's not moving fast. I keep expecting Mrs. Dorio to make an announcement that they've traced the website to Reenzie, or Reenzie herself to make a mistake and let the truth slip, but nothing like that happens. If anything, people's Autumn-hate seems to grow. Reenzie on crutches was a one-day novelty; there's enough dirt on *Winter of My Discontent* to keep everyone reading and furious for the rest of the school year.

It's an ADAPT day, so I leave lunch early. I want to be the first one in the black box. That way I can grab a seat in a far corner and segregate myself before the rest of the group does it for me. I plug earbuds into my phone, close my eyes, and listen to music while I wait.

Someone pulls out the right earbud. I turn and see Sean next to me. He puts the bud in his own ear.

"I didn't peg you as someone into Beethoven," he says, nodding to the beat.

"Huh? This is—" I realize he's joking and I yank the ear-bud back.

"You're hilarious." I turn off the music. "How's Reenzie?"

"She's okay. I'm doing what I can to make it easier for her."

"You're her angel," I say, sounding more sarcastic than I intend to. "I mean, she's lucky to have you," I amend, shrugging.

Sean shrugs back. "She and Trevor broke up, so I'm her go-to guy. It's good, though. She'd do the same for me."

As always, I'm amazed that his Reenzie and my Reenzie are housed in the same body.

The seats are starting to fill. It's almost time to start. Sean leans closer and asks if I'll come watch track practice again, but I don't want to sit in the middle of that many enemies. Especially not after what J.J. told me—that people think I used track practices to spy and get dirt.

"I can't," I say simply, and I can tell by the way his forehead creases that he thinks I'm upset. I guess I am, a little.

"Things have been kind of crazy the last couple of days," he says, "but I want to apologize. I was a total jerk on Monday, about the website. I thought about it a lot and I know it wasn't you."

"Thanks . . . but it kind of sucks that you had to think about it a lot first. Especially after the Formal. I hoped you'd know me better than that."

Sean doesn't seem to know how to respond. Just as well.

ADAPT is starting. He snags me afterward and catches my arm before I can walk away. "Can I text you later?"

The minute he touches me, my heart starts jumping. I'm not happy he doubted me, but I'm not ready to give up on him either.

"That'd be great," I say, smiling at him.

He does, and things with Sean and me get better. We text or talk every night. We just don't hang out, because he's busy with track and helping Reenzie and I like to stay as removed from her as possible so I'm not available for retaliation.

People are still talking trash about me, so clearly the journal hasn't done its job yet. Maybe this is one of those wishes it doesn't want to grant. I'd try something new, but even though Eddy didn't say so, I get the idea the journal isn't a multitasker. If I make another wish, I believe it'll cancel the one still out there, which I don't want to do.

One plus is that I'm drowning in schoolwork, including a paper on *Hamlet* due at the end of next week. That keeps me busy from the end of school till bedtime every night, and all through the weekend. On Monday, I'm still way behind on it, and at the end of the school day I tell Amalita I'll probably be up all night to make a dent in it.

"But you'll take a break at nine-fifty-five, right?" Amalita asks breathlessly.

"Why?"

"*Estas bromeando?* That's when *Pop Star* is announcing

160

the winner of the Kyler Leeds contest! Don't you want to hear them announce my name?"

"I'd love it," I say brightly. "Not gonna happen."

"You have no faith, Autumn," Amalita says, making a *tsk-tsk* sound. "Watch and see. Plus, you want to watch anyway. He tweeted that he's making a 'surprise' appearance on the show to announce the winner himself."

Admittedly, that's worth a homework break. I plan to go downstairs and turn on the TV right before he comes on, but at nine o'clock, Mom knocks on my door and peeks in.

"Aren't you coming downstairs?" she asks hopefully. "*Pop Idol* is on. I heard the magnificent Kyler Leeds himself will be there."

"Yeah, but not until the last five minutes," I say, impressed that she knows this. "I'll be down then."

"Come on, Autumn. Erick and I are already down there. I made popcorn with extra butter, just how you like it. . . ."

I lean back in my desk chair and stretch my arms over my head. "I can't believe you're bribing me with buttered popcorn." And it's totally working. Now I totally have a popcorn craving.

"Just join us. Family time on the couch. It'll be fun."

I follow her downstairs and grab a spot at the end of the couch. Schmidt's next to me and lays his head in my lap. Erick's on the other side of the dog, and Mom has a spot next to him. She hands me a big bowl of popcorn before she sits down herself.

The show's ridiculous. None of the five remaining contestants is any good, and the judges' comments have nothing to do with the performances. It's like they're watching a totally different show. The three of us heckle back. We shout comments the entire time and make each other laugh so hard I nearly choke on my popcorn.

It feels good to sit together and be goofy. We used to do it all the time back in Stillwater. I don't think we've had one evening like this since we moved here. I'm actually bummed when Kyler Leeds comes on, because it means the show's almost over.

"And now it's time for the moment we've all been waiting for," the host announces.

"When Kyler Leeds admits he lip-synchs all his songs," Erick says.

"You're just jealous that he's out of puberty," I say.

"Shut up," Erick says.

"Autumn, your brother is moving through puberty right on schedule."

I laugh out loud. Erick sinks low in the couch.

On the TV, the host stands next to Kyler. There's a giant screen behind them.

"We received millions of entries for the Night of Dreams contest," he continues, "all of which have been entered into a computer randomizer."

The screen bounces unintelligibly with snippets of print shuffling around lightning-fast.

"When Kyler presses this button," the host hands Kyler

a small clicker, "the randomizer will stop on one lucky winner. That winner and the guest of their choice will spend a Night of Dreams with Kyler Leeds! Everyone who entered, good luck!"

"Yes, good luck, everyone," Kyler agrees in his ridiculously cute British accent, "and thank you so much for all your entries. I'm truly honored by all the love and support."

"And the money you spend on my boring music," Erick adds.

"Shut up," I hiss. "He's honored by me."

"Here we go. . . ." Kyler holds up the button. "Even though you know I wish I could spend the night with each and every one of you, there can be only one lucky winner."

Mom frowns. "I'm not sure that's appropriate."

"Three . . . two . . . one!" Kyler presses the button and a single name and place fills the screen behind him in huge block letters.

AUTUMN FALLS
Aventura, FL

An instant later my cell phone starts ringing.
And it doesn't stop.

16

"Our winner is Autumn Falls of Aventura, Florida!"

Kyler Leeds just said my name. In his adorable British accent. On television.

The camera comes in close on Kyler's face. It's like he's speaking directly to me—mainly because he is. "Autumn," he says, looking straight into my eyes via the television, "I'll be seeing you this Saturday, just five days away. I can't wait to meet you, and I know we'll have a true Night of Dreams."

I'm dying. Kyler Leeds is talking to me. Kyler Leeds is going to *come hang with* me.

"Autumn!" Mom screams. "You won!" She pulls me off the couch and into her arms. "I can't believe it! You won!"

"I didn't win," I say, waves of astonishment pouring over me. "I mean, I couldn't have. I didn't *enter*."

"I entered for you," Mom admits excitedly. She fans herself with her hand. "I did it the night you went to see

Eddy. I knew you couldn't possibly win out of all the millions of people who entered, but I had this strange feeling you would, and now you did! It's so exciting! Aren't you excited?" She takes a deep gulp of air. "I think I might faint!"

"Aren't you going to answer your phone?" Erick asks. "It's giving me a headache."

I'm in such shock I barely noticed, but my phone hasn't paused for more than a second since Kyler Leeds said my name.

Kyler. Leeds. Said. My. Name.

"Amalita?" I answer.

All I hear are screams in my ear. When she pauses for breath I try again.

"Ames?"

More screams.

This goes on for a good five minutes, and she's so loud Mom and Erick can hear her. I put the phone on speaker, take it upstairs, shut the door, flop down on my bed, and wait until the screams meld into a tumble of Spanish, English, and possibly Dolphin.

"First of all," she says when she can speak coherently, "you *lied* to me. You said you didn't enter."

"I didn't lie. My mom entered for me."

"Second of all, I will forgive you for that lie, but only if you bring me as your guest."

"As my guest?"

"*Estúpida!* To the Night of Dreams! You and *the guest of your choice* won a Night of Dreams with Kyler Leeds!"

"Ohhhh, and you think I'm going to take you."

"Don't mess with me, Autumn," she says semi-hysterically. "Your only other acceptable option would be Jenna, and you already told me she hates Kyler. Girlfriend has no taste, but I love her for it and will murder you in your sleep if you bring anyone else."

"Aw, that's so sweet."

"I'm not kidding, Autumn. This is Kyler Leeds. No jury would convict me."

"Ames, seriously—of course I'm bringing you."

And the screams begin again.

The entire time we've been talking, my call waiting has been beeping in my ear. I've been ignoring it, but it's finally so annoying that I check to see who it is.

"Ames, stop screaming, you need to hear this. You'll never believe who's on the other line."

She gasps. "It's Kyler Leeds, isn't it? *Dios mío*, if you're on with him, and I'm on with you, it's like *I'm on with Kyler Leeds!*"

"It's Reenzie."

"Reenzie Tresca?" Amalita shrieks. "She's calling to kiss up. She thinks if she's nice to you she'll have a shot at Kyler Leeds."

"She can't be that stupid," I say. "There's no way I'd ever take her."

"Not stupid, sneaky," Amalita corrects.

"Not even sneaky," I say, "obvious. I'm going to tell her it won't work."

I'm about to click over when Amalita gasps. "Don't! This is perfect! This is exactly what we've been waiting for."

"What do you mean?"

"Revenge. Talk to Reenzie. Let her think she has a chance at Kyler Leeds. Act like you're *cuates* and let her spend the next five days getting all excited and let her buy a new dress and do her hair and nails and let her tell everyone she's going, then drop her at the last minute. Squash her like a bug."

I have to admit I like it. It's nowhere near as evil as anything she's done to me, but it turns her own game against her and will make her look beautifully stupid in front of everyone.

"That's good," I say. "But isn't it a little suspicious if I start acting like her best friend?"

"She doesn't think you'll be suspicious that she's doing the same thing to you," Amalita says urgently. "Plus, it's Reenzie. Worked on Taylor, she'll think it's working on you."

The phone is beeping in my ear again. I check the screen. "She's back," I say.

"Take the call. Rope her in. Call me after. Revenge!"

She hangs up and I click over. "Hello?"

"Autumn? Hey, it's Reenzie. I hope you don't mind, I got your number from Sean."

"Um, sure. What's up?"

"Not much. I was just thinking . . . Sean's been talking about you a lot, and I can tell he'd like it if we hung out.

Are you around tomorrow after school? I thought maybe you could hang at track practice and come back to my place after. Sean will drive us. We could watch a movie or something."

I go for hard-to-get. Less suspicious. "I can't watch you guys at track. I have a paper due."

"Maybe we could swing by your house and get you? Then you could work for a while first. I really feel like I messed up with you, and I want to make it better."

Does she honestly think anyone would buy this? The only real way she could make things better is to confess what an evil, scheming witch she is in front of the entire school.

Suddenly, I gasp.

I drop the phone on my bed.

Oh my God.

That's what I wished for. I wished for the whole school to know the truth about Reenzie.

This is how that wish is coming true.

That's why I won a contest it was impossible for me to win. Kyler Leeds didn't pick my name, the journal did. And now the journal's giving me a five-day window to get close to Reenzie. To catch her off guard. To get into her house.

To get justice.

"Autumn?" I hear Reenzie's voice from my phone. "You there?"

"Yeah," I say when I've picked the phone back up.

"Sounds great. I'll see you after school tomorrow. Sean knows the address."

Reenzie's thrilled and babbles in my ear about random things I guess I'm supposed to be happy she's sharing, but all I hear is the clock that just started ticking down in my head to Saturday.

If Reenzie weren't so evil, I could almost feel sorry for her. She's on borrowed time, and she has no idea.

17

When I check my phone the next morning, it's clogged with texts. Most of them are from numbers I don't know. I scroll through and see a lot of Hey, Autumn, it's [insert name of classmate/ex-classmate/distant relative], followed by congratulations on winning the Kyler Leeds contest, then a request to get together or talk soon so we can catch up. The "soon" is almost always in caps.

I'm not sure what's more surprising: that all these people somehow got my cell phone number, or that a lot of the texts are from people who have been actively bombarding me with venom at school. Even Shayla McConkle sent a

Let's get together SOON!

I delete all the texts except one from Jenna:

Everyone you have ever known is calling me. Congratulations!!! When you meet him, please give him permanent laryngitis from me. Thx!

I will never understand how Jenna can't adore Kyler Leeds. It's really her only flaw.

My email is equally full. I go wild with the Delete button and nearly erase the one email I actually want. Chills dance up my spine and I stop breathing for a second.

It's from *Kyler Leeds*.

At least, it seems that way, but when I open it I realize it's only sort of from Kyler. It's really from Donovan, his assistant. Donovan's coordinating the Night of Dreams. He needs to confirm my home address and that he can pick up me and a friend there at six p.m. on Saturday. There's also a bunch of forms I have to print out and sign or get signed—a parental permission slip and something that says I'm cool with being filmed.

I'm shaking a little. I've been so caught up in how I'm going to use the Night of Dreams to nail Reenzie, I didn't even think about the reality. In four days I'm going out with Kyler Leeds. I, Autumn Falls, am going out for the night with *Kyler Leeds*!

"Carrie Amernick called me last night," J.J. says when we meet up. "She wants to know how to become your new best friend so she can meet Kyler Leeds."

"Did you give her the secret formula?"

"Only if the secret formula is 'Amalita will shave you bald if you think of trying to snag her spot.'"

"It's a good thing you guys aren't together," I say. "Girls don't like when you lie to them."

"I'm not lying," J.J. says. "Amalita would literally break into Carrie's house and shave her head."

"True," I say, "but you lied about me taking Amalita. At least, Carrie will think so."

"I've already blasted through one cryptogram this morning," J.J. says, "so maybe you could just tell me what you mean."

I tell him Amalita's plan to promise Reenzie the night, then dump her at the last minute. "But that's just the beginning," I continue. "I've added another layer. In her misguided attempt to become my best friend, Reenzie has invited me to her house, where I can secretly gather evidence."

"Evidence?"

"That she posted the picture of me on the student portal. That she started the rumors about why I left Maryland. That she's the one behind *Winter of My Discontent*."

"The site's down, by the way."

"Of course it is," I say. "Because Reenzie knows that I know that she did it, and she wants me to think we're friends now. How do you know it's down? Do you cruise it regularly?"

"Never more than the once," he says. "But sadly, Carrie does. She told me it's down. She's disappointed there won't be more updates, but assures me she cut and pasted all the best dirt into another file."

"You really went out with her?"

"She has other redeeming qualities," J.J. says.

"Two of them, maybe?" I ask, rolling my eyes.

We're at school now, and as we head for the door I instinctively move closer to J.J. I get tripped, pushed, and cursed far less violently when I'm next to someone than when I'm alone.

Then I remember the slew of texts and emails from all my new "friends." I walk ahead of J.J. and throw open the doors.

"Hi, Autumn!"

"Hey!"

"Congratulations!"

"Autumn! I'm so excited for you!"

"Are you dying? I'd be dying!"

The minute I walk in I'm surrounded. Huge smiles on everyone's faces. Hugs from people who have no reason to believe they'd be welcome in my personal space.

I won't lie. It feels great. I know it's meaningless. I know it's only because I have something they want. Still, I bask in it. And when Sofia Brooks links her arm through mine and asks me if I've decided who I'm taking on the Night of Dreams, I'm thrilled that Amalita's and my plan requires me to say no.

The throng of admirers walks me all the way to homeroom. When I walk in, I see Sean and Reenzie next to one another. There's a free seat next to each of them and I'm dying to take the one by Sean, but Reenzie's waving me over, a huge grin on her face. I sit next to her.

"Congratulations!" she says. "I just heard about you and Kyler Leeds!"

"You didn't know?" I ask. "'Cause you called me last night right after it was announced, so—"

"No!" Reenzie says. "Total coincidence!"

I catch Sean's eye. I can tell from the look on his face that even he knows she's lying, but he seems more amused than bothered. We share a smirk at Reenzie's expense. I wouldn't say it feels as good as sharing a kiss, but it's up there.

"So do you know who you're bringing?" Reenzie asks me.

"Not yet," I say. "I need to decide soon, I guess. It's just four days away."

"Crazy," Reenzie says. "Well, I will just put out there that I'm a huge Kyler Leeds fan, and totally willing to go anywhere, even in a full leg cast."

"Maybe he could sign it," I say. "Then after it comes off you could sell it."

"Or keep it forever to help me remember a fabulous Night of Dreams," she says. "If I went, I mean."

Lunch is a trip. I come out of the Tube with my tray and it's like I'm at a rock concert—all the arms waving in the air. Only they're not cheering for a band, they're calling for me to come join their groups and be their friend for the day. Or maybe the next four days.

I smile at everyone but still beeline for Amalita, Jack, and J.J. I'm almost to them when I hear Reenzie shouting my name. Amalita and I lock eyes; then I completely change paths.

"Reenzie! Hey!" I say as I head her way.

"Are you kidding me?" Amalita trails behind me. "You're blowing me off for her? Don't mess with me, Autumn. You will not like what happens when you mess with me!"

It's hard not to laugh.

"Sorry about that," I say when I get to Reenzie. She's sitting on a folding chair like a queen on her favorite spot of lawn with Taylor, Sean, and a group of other people I recognize from track. Zach isn't around. I wonder if he and Taylor broke up. Then I wonder whether if they did, it was because Reenzie and Trevor broke up and Taylor felt she had to follow suit.

"Don't worry about it," Reenzie says. "All due respect, I know she's your friend, but she's a little crazy. Come sit." She points to the ground next to her. "Scooch over," she tells Taylor. "Autumn needs room."

Taylor obediently moves over, but she doesn't look happy about it.

"So Sean's been saying great things about you," Reenzie says, "but none of us know you that well. Time to fill us in. Autumn Falls, ten words or less. Go."

The whole crowd stares at me. I can feel the spotlight blazing down. I suddenly hate Amalita's and my plan.

"Bitingly funny beauty with a secret passion for the game of football," Sean says.

I don't know if it's what he said or the fact that he saved me, but I may well love him.

"That's twelve words," I say, "but if you get rid of 'the game of' and replace 'secret passion' with 'wild indifference,' you're good."

Now a bunch of people jump in to try to convince me of the awesomeness of football. None of them succeeds, but it breaks the ice, and soon we're all talking like we've hung out forever. I have to remind myself it isn't real. If Reenzie hadn't pulled me under her wing to get to Kyler Leeds, all these people except Sean would still hate me. They probably *do* still hate me; they're just acting nice for Reenzie's sake.

After school I go home and try to make headway on *Hamlet,* but I'm distracted. I keep texting with Amalita about the best way to find evidence at Reenzie's house.

Don't stress, she writes. Exposing her great, but original plan still works on its own.

She's right, but exposing Reenzie is what I wished for in the journal, and I know I can make it happen. I just have to figure out how.

Sean calls when he's about to pull up at my house. When I run out to meet him, I see Reenzie wave from the passenger seat, so I climb into the back.

"Hey!" Reenzie says, nodding. "Sorry we're a little late. Practice ran long." She blew out her breath. "Coach wants me there even though all I can do is sit and watch."

"How long will you be in the cast?" I ask.

"Six weeks. Sucks."

I feel incredibly guilty, then shake it off. I have a mission to accomplish.

"So we're going to your house?" I ask.

"We were," Reenzie says, "but I had a better idea. I think you'll like it. It's a little cheesy but very fun."

"Hanging out at the house sounds fun," I say hesitantly, wondering what she has in her evil mind.

"Well, this is *more* fun," Reenzie says, flashing me a smile.

I catch Sean's eye in the rearview mirror. He shrugs. "Usually best to just go along with Reenzie once she's set on something."

"Believe him," Reenzie says. "He's spent his whole life learning that lesson."

Sean rolls his eyes. They have such an easy rapport. It's like they really are brother and sister.

A little while later, Sean pulls up near a high school parking lot filled with carnival rides. It's already dark, and everything blinks in yellow, red, and blue. Through the window I can see the top of a high Ferris wheel, a rocking pirate ship, and one of those insane giant arms that rises high into the air, then spins a wheel of gondolas filled with people who don't value their lives.

"We're going here?" I ask, dubious. "But you're on crutches."

"I'll manage," Reenzie says, then reaches out to grab Sean as he opens his door. "Not you," she tells him. "You drop us off, my mom will pick us up later."

"You're not serious," Sean says, looking from me to Reenzie.

"I am!" Reenzie insists. "You said you want me to get along better with Autumn, right? This is our time to bond."

"Give me a second," he says, then gets out of the car and opens my door so I can climb out and join him. He stands very close and speaks in a low voice that reverberates through me.

"Do you mind?" he asks. "'Cause if you mind, I'll stay."

"It's fine," I say, forcing myself to smile. "Really."

"Cool," he says. "Because she's right. I know she hasn't been your favorite person, but it would be great if you guys got along."

"And if we don't?" I ask, not sure I want to know the answer. "Is that a deal breaker?"

Sean laughs. "I don't choose who I like based on Reenzie's opinions. But it was really nice, all of us hanging out together today. I'd like to do it more. I like being around you."

He leans down and kisses me. I forget about the plan, the Night of Dreams, everything except the way he feels against me. I wrap my arms around his neck . . .

. . . then leap back as his car horn blares.

Reenzie leans across to the driver's side to shout out the window, "Save it for later! Crippled girl waiting in the car!"

Sean smiles apologetically, then goes around to help Reenzie. I'm still in a daze. By the time I snap out of it,

Sean has driven away and I'm alone with Reenzie Tresca in front of a high school carnival.

"You ready?" she asks.

I should back out. I should say I don't feel good, call my mom, and get a ride home. Sean likes me. He won't like me if I lead Reenzie on and then dump her on Saturday right before the Night of Dreams.

But Reenzie deserves it. And if I also manage to dig up the proof I want, then Sean will *know* she deserves it, and he'll understand.

I give Reenzie my friendliest smile. "Let's do it."

That evening I have a front-row seat at the Reenzie Show, and I have to admit it's impressive. As someone who so far has dealt mainly with Mr. Hyde, I'm blown away by the power of Dr. Jekyll. Reenzie chats with the guy at the ticket booth for all of two minutes, and he not only lets us in for free but slips us a massive stack of ride tickets. She schmoozes every ride operator until they let her on, even though I'm pretty sure it's illegal for her to ride in a full leg cast. Guys buy us cotton candy and popcorn, try to win us stuffed animals, and spring for us to mush into the photo booth so we'll have a souvenir of the evening.

I'm even charmed by Reenzie. I know what she really is, and I still can't help it. It's like she can flip a switch and turn on this electric charisma that not only makes her shine brighter than anyone else, but also makes me shine brighter because I'm with her. I glow by extension. I know, I *know* what she's all about, but I still spend the whole evening laughing with her, screaming with her on the rides—I even cling to her on the roller coaster, like she's the one who'd save me if anything went wrong.

"I had an amazing time," I tell her at the end of the night, and I'm stunned by how true that is.

"Me too," she says. "We should hang out more often."

"We should," I agree. "In fact . . . are you doing anything Saturday?"

"Saturday?"

"Yeah. It's the night of the Kyler Leeds thing. I know you said you're a fan. Do you think you'd want to go with me?"

"Really? I'd love it! Thank you, Autumn!"

She hugs me as best she can while leaning on her crutches, and when she raves to her mom on the way home about our fantastic night at the carnival, what a great new friend I am, and the incredible time we're going to have with *Kyler Leeds* on Saturday night, I almost feel a little bit guilty.

Almost.

18

I think I just threw up in my mouth.

That's the message I get back from Amalita when I text her a picture of the Reenzie/Autumn photo booth strip.

AUTUMN: Revenge requires suffering.

AMALITA: You look like you're having a
good time with her. Tell me you didn't
have a good time with her.

AUTUMN: Can't lie—very fun. But very fake.
Bummed I didn't get into her house though.
Maybe tonight.

"I heard you're taking Reenzie to the Night of Dreams with Kyler Leeds," J.J. says when I meet him on the way to school.

"Carrie Amernick?" I ask.

"She's furious. She understood Amalita, but since it's Reenzie, she figures she had a shot. She blames me."

"Is that one of her redeeming qualities?"

"I don't know," J.J. says. "I do seem to surround myself with angry women."

"I'm justifiably angry," I say. "It's different."

Carrie Amernick is not the only one who already knows Reenzie's my friend of choice for the Night of Dreams. Unlike yesterday, I'm not swarmed by admirers when I walk into school. People still smile and wave and say hi, though. Maybe they're hoping for an autograph. Or they're hedging their bets in case Kyler and I hit it off and become best friends.

When I turn the corner, my stomach flips.

Sean's standing by my locker.

He has his hands in his pockets and shifts uncomfortably, but he smiles when he sees me.

"Hi," I say.

"Hey."

"Sorry you weren't with us last night," I say. "It was a lot of fun."

"I heard. I heard you even asked her to the Kyler Leeds thing."

"Yeah, I did."

"Okay, so I have to ask . . . why?"

"What do you mean?"

"It's just weird," he says. "I mean, believe me, I'm glad you're hanging out and it's good, but it's not like it's a secret that she wasn't interested before you won that contest."

"I know."

"So . . . why Reenzie?"

Lying isn't the best way to start what I hope will be a long and wonderful relationship, but the truth is clearly not an option.

"You don't want me to take her?" I ask.

"No, it's cool if you want to. It's just, I don't know . . . I don't want you to feel like you have to do that for me. 'Cause you don't."

If I had any confidence that he'd be okay with it, I'd throw my arms around him and kiss him in the middle of the hall.

He's protecting me. How sweet is that?

"Wow," I say, smiling at him. I wish I could tell him the truth, but I just can't. "Can that ego actually fit inside a football helmet?"

"It's a tight squeeze," he admits.

"It doesn't matter why Reenzie and I started hanging out," I say. "We're friends now. I'm taking her because I want to take her."

It's disturbing how easily I lie to Sean. I only feel worse when he smiles, takes my hand, and walks me to homeroom.

He believes me. And he really likes me. If I dump Reenzie at the last minute after this, he'll never want anything to do with me.

I could actually take Reenzie. I can even imagine an evening with her and Kyler Leeds. She'd be her charming, fabulous self, I'd seem just as charming in her presence, and Kyler would have so much fun he'd probably come back to visit us every time he was in town. Maybe he'd even go out with Reenzie, and she'd be so grateful she'd forgive me for stealing Sean away from her.

I could do it . . . but it would destroy Amalita. J.J. and Jack would hate me for it. And wouldn't taking Reenzie mean I'm okay with everything she did to me?

Yeah, it would. And I'm not.

Evidence. It's the only way this can work out.

I take a step in that direction during lunch. I'm with Reenzie and her friends again, in the place of honor at Reenzie's side. Sean's next to me. Taylor, I notice, sits across from us, as far away as she can get. I ask Reenzie if she's up for hanging out again this afternoon. I'm hoping she suggests her house because I'm not sure how to invite myself there, but instead she says she already has it planned: we're going dress shopping for our Big Night.

"That sounds fun, but I wasn't actually planning on getting a new dress," I say, taking a spoonful of yogurt. "I'm going to wear the same dress I wore for Winter Formal."

"You looked really pretty in that dress," Sean says, making me feel awesome.

"Unacceptable," Reenzie says, waving away my idea as if it was the worst thing she'd ever heard. "This is Kyler Leeds. You need something new and spectacular."

"Did you see her at Winter Formal?" Sean asks. "Spectacular's covered."

"I remember the other day you said something about going to your place and watching a movie," I say, trying to work that angle. "That sounded fun."

"But not as much fun as what we actually ended up doing, right?" she asks. Then she tells the rest of the circle, "Autumn and I crashed the Deerfield High carnival."

"You went to that with Autumn?" Taylor asks, looking crestfallen. "You said we were going to go."

"Did I?" Reenzie asks. "Shoot. Well, you should definitely check it out. It was fantastic."

Taylor looks miserable. If I could do it subtly I'd snap a picture and text it to Amalita with the caption Dumper Becomes Dumpee.

Justice abounds.

I can't talk Reenzie out of dress shopping that afternoon. She doesn't want to go to the mall; instead her mom picks me up at my house after track practice and drives us to her favorite boutiques. Reenzie tries on dresses at all of them—slowly, easing each one over her cast and around her crutches—and at the end opts for something from the very first store. I try things on, but I don't buy anything. I'm good with what I have; plus, everything is too expensive.

Today is nowhere near as much fun as yesterday. I tell myself it's because Reenzie already has the Night of Dreams invitation and isn't trying as hard, but the truth is it's not Reenzie at all, it's me. I'm starting to feel as if my grand plan for justice is going to blow up in my face and kill anything good with Sean. I desperately don't want that to happen, but I don't know how to stop it. I can't make Reenzie take me to her house. And honestly, even if I get in there, what makes me think I'll find any proof of what she did to me?

"I really wanted to take you girls out to dinner, but it's getting so late," Reenzie's mom says as we climb back into the car with Reenzie's new dress. "Tell you what. Mr. Tresca and I have plans tomorrow, but, Autumn, I want you to come home with Reenzie after practice on Friday and I'll make you dinner. How does that sound?"

I smile. "Wow, that's so nice of you," I say. Reenzie grins over at me.

It also sounds like the journal is still hard at work on my wish for justice. I've got to have faith it will help me find what I need.

19

I print out the garbled disaster that is currently my *Hamlet* paper during one of my free periods, and spend the rest of the day making little edits and notes all over it. And when I'm not reading it for the fiftieth time, I'm with Reenzie, Sean, and their crowd.

Over the past few days I've gotten so used to people *not* glaring at me that it's painfully obvious when Taylor won't stop. She doesn't say anything to me—or to anyone, really—just laser-blasts me with her eyes or pouts down at her food.

I ignore it.

I excuse myself long before lunch ends so I can slip back into the library, but I barely get anything done before a voice hisses over my shoulder.

"You have your own friends. You don't need to try and steal mine."

I turn around to face her. Her jaw is tight and her eyes burn.

This is weird. It's one thing to get all sulky when she's ignored at lunch, but following me to the library? Does she not realize Reenzie's only hanging out with me for the Kyler Leeds date?

If not, I'm certainly not going to be the one to enlighten her. Instead I say, "So you're upset because your friend's dumping you for someone new? Isn't that just poetic justice?"

"Believe me, Reenzie won't care about you after Saturday," Taylor says coldly. "And no, it wouldn't be 'poetic justice.' I don't know what Amalita told you, but I did *not* dump her. I just didn't want to be surgically attached to her, and she couldn't handle that. Which is pretty funny since she had no problems sliding you right into the slot I left behind."

"Wait . . . are you upset that I'm hanging out with Reenzie, or with Amalita, Jack, and J.J.?"

Taylor rolls her eyes and shakes her head as though I don't understand anything at all, then stalks away.

I can't deal with whatever insanity is going on in her head. Hamlet and I both have more pressing plans that require my immediate attention. I stay in the library as long as I can, then go back home the minute school ends, plant my butt in front of the computer, and don't move until two a.m. Then, finally, with my paper done, I have the chance to sleep, perchance to dream.

After only four hours of sleep I should be running on fumes. Instead I'm buzzing. Not only do I have in my bag a fully completed and just-this-side-of-brilliant *Hamlet* paper, but tonight is the night I go to Reenzie's and find the evidence that will bring her down.

Jack and Amalita run outside to meet J.J. and me just before we walk into the school. They look around before they speak, as if to make sure no one is watching.

"You'll want this," Jack says, as if we're on some super-secret spy mission.

He slips something into my hand. I look at it.

"A tiny rubber Wonder Woman?" I ask.

"A flash drive," Jack says, "that yes, happens to be hidden inside a tiny rubber Wonder Woman."

"For tonight," Amalita says.

"Best place to find evidence is on her computer," Jack says. "Hopefully it's not password protected."

"Most likely her computer's in her room," Amalita says. "You'll have to get there alone with time to check everything out."

"Anything you find, drag it onto the flash drive," Jack says.

"And don't get caught," J.J. says. "Ramifications for getting caught, very bad."

"Mortifying, for sure," I say, imagining Reenzie finding me alone in her room for no good reason.

"Embarrassment a minor issue," J.J. says. "Worst-case scenario, she finds you downloading files, it's stealing. Might be a tough prosecution in court, but definitely enough to get you expelled."

"In *court*?" I ask. "Like an actual court of law?"

"Sure, but that would never in a million years actually happen," Amalita says.

"Agreed," J.J. says. "Far more likely her mom would turn you in to Mrs. Dorio. Hence, expulsion."

"That makes me feel much better," I mutter.

"You don't have to worry about it because it *won't happen*," Amalita says. "You'll be careful. And any time you start to freak out, remember why you're doing this." She turns her phone screen to me. On it is a page from the *Winter of My Discontent* site.

"It's back up?" I ask.

"No. I took a screen shot for motivation. I have this too." She scrolls around, then holds up the picture from the student portal: the lump on my forehead, the delusionally vacant eyes, the dazed pucker.

"Right," I say, filled with a renewed sense of purpose. "I'm going to nail her."

By now I'm late for homeroom, though naturally Reenzie saved me a seat. I can't look her in the eye. She doesn't seem to notice.

The school day drags horrifically. Lunch is a highlight. I sprawl next to Sean on the lawn like yesterday, and he sits so close we lean against each other the whole time. We're not quite together, but we're definitely not *not* together.

There are worse places to be.

Since my paper's finished, and since I'm going with Reenzie and Sean after practice, I head down to the track after school for the first time in ages. This time I sit with Reenzie, right at the edge of the track. She's intently focused on the pole-vaulters, and gives me a running commentary of every little improvement in someone's approach, or glitch in their plant and takeoff. I can tell her teammates know she's talking about them, but they don't seem to mind. In fact, they want her opinion. After each vault they look to her, right after they get feedback from their coach.

When the vaulters aren't working, Reenzie turns her attention to the ever-widening circle of people who plop down around us to talk about Kyler Leeds and the Night of Dreams. Everyone knows it's this Saturday, and it's obvious they've been talking to Reenzie the last couple days, because they know every detail, including what Reenzie's dress and all her accessory options look like. Reenzie's practically a celebrity herself, basking in the glow of their jealousy and generously telling everyone she'd *love* to get them the tiny little signature/recorded message/picture they want, but if she does it for one person she'd have to do it for everyone, and that simply wouldn't be fair.

Listening to her hold court, I wonder . . . The plan is that Reenzie will look and feel like a fool when she ends up *not* going on the Night of Dreams, but for the first time I wonder if she'll look foolish or I'll look evil for dropping her. Small beads of sweat dot my forehead as I think about this.

It doesn't matter. The crowd happy to gather around me now is the same group that happily believed the worst about me before. They don't know the truth.

Yet.

After practice, Sean drives Reenzie and me to her house. Her cast gives her automatic shotgun, but I'm happier shoved in the back. This way they won't expect me to talk, and right now my heart is thudding so violently I know they'd hear it in my voice.

I reach down and feel the little Wonder Woman in my shorts pocket. This is it. Sometime tonight I'm going to commit an illegal act. Two of them, actually. Breaking and entering, and theft.

Except I'm not breaking into anything. Reenzie's inviting me into her home. I'm entering into her computer files, but that's not illegal so much as generally amoral and not okay. As for any files I grab, I'm only *copying* them. It's not theft if I don't take anything away.

Besides, it's all for a good cause. Robin Hood never went to jail for stealing from the rich, right? Wait—was Robin Hood even real or just a story? I pull out my phone to do a quick search, but we're at Reenzie's house before I find out.

Her home is gorgeous, but it's also enormous. When

Mrs. Tresca opens the door and we pile into the foyer, I'm blinded by the marble floors, the spiral staircase, and the gigantic crystal chandelier. I can't even imagine how many rooms there are, but I can easily imagine myself scrambling hopelessly into each one while whatever alone time I manage to carve out slips away.

"Your house is so beautiful, Reenzie," I say. "Can you give me a tour?"

Reenzie looks down at her giant purple cast, then back up at me. "Seriously?"

"I'll take you, Autumn," Mrs. Tresca says as Reenzie tugs on Sean's arm. "You are staying, Sean, right?"

Sean answers her, but he's looking right at me. "Yeah, sure."

I'm thrilled and devastated. Of course, I'm light-headed knowing Sean wants to spend time with me, but I'd feel much more secure wandering into Reenzie's room when the only person really aware I was missing was on crutches.

My mind is racing as Mrs. Tresca starts the tour, but luckily she's a talker and I don't have to say much of anything. I do, however, find out some salient facts: (1) Reenzie's room is on the second floor. (2) There is indeed a computer on her desk. (3) The door to the room is left slightly ajar, thus making it blissfully easy to get inside and have some protection from prying eyes while there.

"Do you have any pets?" I ask as Mrs. Tresca leads me back downstairs after the tour. "I love animals," I add when I realize she might think it's an odd non sequitur.

"I do too, but Mr. Tresca's very allergic," she says. "No pets."

Good. Nothing to bark or meow if I'm someplace I shouldn't be.

The screening room is back on the first floor, and the name is fancier than the space. It's not like it's a mini movie theater, just a large room with blackout shades, a massive-screen TV on one wall, and several couches with sections that open out to recliners. Reenzie's on one of those sections, tilted back in the cushions with her broken leg stretched in front of her.

"I promise, just one more," Sean says. My eyes flicker to the *SpongeBob* episode on the screen.

"We're going to miss the opening part," Reenzie whines, then turns to me. "*Mean Girls* is on," she says by way of explanation. "I love that movie."

I bet.

I sit down next to Sean on the couch and watch as they fight good-naturedly over the remote, switching the channel every few minutes.

"Are you guys hungry?" Reenzie asks. "Dinner will be ready soon, but I think we've got chips and salsa in the cabinet."

"No thanks," I say too loudly. "My stomach's kind of bothering me."

My stomach is fine. We could be watching *SpongeBob*, *Mean Girls*, or CNN. To me, it's just background noise. Even though Sean sidles close to me and rests his arm across the back of my couch cushion so he basically has his arm around me, I can't relax and enjoy it. At last Sean and Reenzie get sucked into some show about real-life ghost hunters. They won't notice if I'm gone for a little while.

"I'm so sorry," I stage-whisper. "Where's the bathroom?"

"Down the hall and make two lefts," Reenzie says.

"Want me to show you?" Sean asks, looking concerned.

"No, I'll be fine."

I walk down the hall and make the left turns. I can hear Mrs. Tresca puttering around in the kitchen, which means everyone in the house is accounted for. As quickly and silently as possible, I race up the stairs and duck into Reenzie's room without touching the door, as if someone might notice even the slightest change in its position.

My thudding heart and gasping breath are way too loud. Someone's going to hear. I stand right behind the door and take deep breaths until I calm down. I leave the lights out and move to Reenzie's desk. When I look toward the door, I can see I'm safely hidden. Still, I can only stay away for so long.

I sit at the desk and tap a computer key. I'm positive I'll get a password screen and this whole thing will be useless, but I don't. The screen saver shudders to a Word doc. I scan a few sentences. Something about *Brave New World*. A paper for her English class.

I check the time: it's 5:05. I can get away with ten minutes, maybe. Fifteen, tops.

What were my friends and I thinking? This is crazy. Even if she has incriminating files, how am I going to find them?

I click the Finder, then Documents. In the search bar I type "Autumn." A list of files comes up and I enlarge them with the space bar to scan through, but none of them has anything to do with me.

Of course not. Who'd be dumb enough to label their libelous files with the name of the person they trashed?

I could search something in the document. Something that she wrote in *Winter of My Discontent*. What did she write?

For the first time I wish she hadn't taken down the site. Amalita!

I quickly text her.

Text me pic of Discontent site ASAP!!!!

Thankfully she's around. I get the picture a second later. I enlarge it and look for a phrase unique enough that it wouldn't be in a lot of other documents.

Really bad choice, or klepto? I type into the search bar. It's from something she wrote about Sofia Brooks. As I type each word, the list of matching documents gets smaller. I'm sure by the time I key in the final question mark I'll come up empty.

But I don't.

One file is left on the list. It's called "Richard III." As I proved with *Hamlet,* I know exactly zilch about Shakespeare, but I'd bet that play is where the "winter of my dis-content" quote appears.

I highlight the file. It was created at the end of January, almost a month before the website went up. I press the space bar to preview it.

It's all the text for the website—the whole list of people with their dirt, right there in front of my eyes.

Oh my God. I forgot how hideous some of this is.

◄ **Evie Watters:** *The closet is so 20th century. We all know already, so come out come out wherever you are.*

◄ **Colin Radnor:** *I'm looking out for your best interests. Breath does not get that noxious without a physiological cause. See a doctor.*

◄ **Robin Prouse:** *We both know why Mr. Edmunds retired early. The question is, did you at least get an A?*

It's way too easy to get lost in the horror. I take one second to text Amalita PAYDIRT!, then pull the tiny rubber Wonder Woman from my pocket. I tear her in half to reveal her plug, then insert it into the USB port.

The computer recognizes the drive. I see it in the Finder. "Wonder Wench." Jack is nothing if not poetic. I highlight the "Richard III" file and I'm about to drag it over when I hear the door creak open.

I freeze.

"Autumn?"

I slowly spin around in the chair.

It's Sean.

I can't move or talk. I am frozen in Reenzie's chair, my hand soldered to her mouse.

"Hi," I finally croak out.

He stares at me. "What are you doing?"

There's nothing playful in his voice. Nothing friendly.

"I . . . What are you doing up here?" I ask, not answering his question. I can't. Telling him the truth would be like stabbing myself with my protractor.

He looks at me with his mouth open, as though he can't believe I asked the question. "You were gone a long time, so I went to check on you. The bathroom was open and you weren't there, so I thought you went looking for another one. Then I heard typing."

I can't fathom why the bathroom would be open. I closed it when I left. Mrs. Tresca must have gone in while I was up here. And how could he think I was gone so long? It's only . . .

I turn and look at Reenzie's computer screen—5:35. Totally lost track of time.

"Autumn." Sean says my name like it disgusts him. "What are you doing?"

In a split second I run through every possible excuse, but they're all insultingly bad.

"I was looking for proof that Reenzie was the one behind the *Winter of My Discontent* website," I blurt out in a desperate rush of words. "I know it was her, and no one believes me, not even you, so I had to find evidence."

Sean looks at me as if he's doing complicated math in his head. He doesn't say anything for a while. When he does speak, his words come slowly, as though he doesn't want to believe they're true.

"Did you . . . Is this the only reason you invited Reenzie to Kyler Leeds? So you could get in here and look through her stuff? Are you even actually taking her?"

I could lie. I could easily lie.

And it would blow up in my face in less than twenty-four hours.

"No," I admit, feeling like a small, pitiful creep. "I'm taking Amalita."

He's speechless. He just stares at me.

"But, Sean, I was right," I quickly say, finding some courage. "I found the proof. Look!"

"I don't want to look. I don't look at other people's things. I don't do that."

"I'm not the evil one here," I protest, scrambling to find the right thing to say.

He lets out a short, bitter laugh. "Are you serious?"

Now I'm blinking back tears. "Yes. This looks pretty bad, but this is different, Sean. It's justice."

He just looks at me and shakes his head. "With all the crap thrown in your face, you were this amazing person who stayed true to herself and had friends who cared about her and did her thing no matter what anyone else thought."

I'm at a loss. The way he's shaking his head makes me feel terrible, like what I did really disappointed him. "That's how you see me?"

"That's how I *saw* you. I was wrong."

"Sean? Autumn?" Reenzie's voice floats up from downstairs. "You guys alive? No making out in the house."

"Down in a second," Sean shouts down, but he keeps his eyes focused on mine.

"Are you going to tell her?" I ask, biting my lip.

"I should," he says. "But no. Not about the computer. But you're going to tell her right now that you aren't taking her to Kyler Leeds. And then you're getting out of this house. And if any of her files show up anywhere else, I'm telling Reenzie, her mom . . . even Mrs. Dorio how you lied and broke into this computer."

My stomach drops and my throat closes up. I could refuse, but then I'd never have a chance with Sean, and part of me is hoping that once he gets over his anger, he'll understand why I did what I did. So I nod, then eject Wonder Woman, put her back together, and slip her in my pocket. I keep hoping Sean will look over my shoulder at the evidence file before I close it, but he never does. When everything's back together I follow him downstairs and back to the screening room. He stands with his arms crossed and waits while I hang my head like a naughty child.

"Reenzie," I say slowly, "I have something to tell you."

The one good thing about having something truly un-bearable happen in your life is that things that would otherwise be horrific aren't so bad.

That said, telling Reenzie is awful. She screams, she insults me, she even stomps her foot—and the whole time Sean just stands stone-still. He doesn't say a word or change his expression once, not even when Mrs. Tresca comes in to see what's going on and Reenzie screams at her to leave. When it's all over, Sean walks me to the door and opens it, waits for me to step outside, then slams it in my face. Never mind that I have no ride home. He doesn't care.

I want to sit down and cry, but more than that, I want to get far away from Reenzie and Sean. I walk a few blocks to the opening of their development, then call my mom to come get me. I don't do anything while I wait. I don't even think. Mom can tell I'm upset when I get into the car, but there's no way I can explain, so I stay silent. At home I don't want to be anything but unconscious. I go right up to bed, tunnel under the covers, and shut out the world.

20

I sleep in. Even when I wake up I refuse to open my eyes. I roll over and breathe deeply into my pillow.

I know it's not working anymore when I can't get Sean's voice out of my head. I keep thinking about what he said. How he saw me for who I am—someone who's had a lot of crap thrown at her but who has stayed true to herself. And because of that, I had friends who cared about me—Sean included—despite anything Reenzie did.

When I think of how he described it, it's kind of like I *was* bringing peace and harmony to my little corner of the world.

I get out of bed, dig my journal out of my bag, and look at my last wish.

> I wish that everyone at that school could find out exactly what Reenzie did to me, and see her for the person she really is.

Was that wish sending me off the track of my mission? Is that why it imploded so horribly?

I pick up a pen and write.

Dear Dad,

It hurts to tell him about what I did. Planning the attack on Reenzie's computer felt daring and kind of Hit-Girl and capital-R Right, but when I imagine Dad reading about it, I know he'd be upset with me.

You gave me this gift, I write, *but I'm not using it to bring peace and harmony. I'm just messing everything up and I don't know how to make it better. I wish I could do the right thing and make you proud.*

I put the journal away and check my phone.

AMALITA: What did you find?

AMALITA: How are you not answering me?

AMALITA: Helloooo???

AMALITA: OMG, did you get caught? Tell me you didn't get caught.

AMALITA: Are you kidding me with this? Text me! Call me! Now!

It goes on from there.

I call her.

"*Autumn!* It's noon and we're seeing Kyler Leeds in exactly six hours! There is no good reason for you not to call until now!"

I give her my good reason.

"*Y que?*" she asks calmly.

"So what?" I repeat incredulously.

"You're looking at the bad side," Amalita says, and I can picture her waving her hand in the air. "Yes, you got caught, we didn't get the evidence, and we can't out Reenzie to the whole school. But you saw it, so *you* know. Sean didn't turn you in, and Reenzie will still have to tell everyone she did not in fact get to meet Kyler Leeds. And by the way—*we do!* This is all *muy buena.*"

"Except Sean hates me," I say miserably.

"Which means you're not a threat to Reenzie anymore and she'll leave you alone! See? *La vida es buena.* Tonight is going to be unbelievable."

I can't convince her that everything didn't turn out perfectly. And then we hang up because we're meeting in a half hour. We have appointments to get our hair done.

Amalita's not wrong, I think as my mom gives me a ride to the salon. Being led on about Kyler, then dumped, is the least Reenzie deserved, especially now that I've seen proof she wrote the website. And tonight I get to spend an evening with the one celebrity I'd give anything in the universe to even stand near for two seconds. Better still, I get to bring along Amalita, my closest friend in Aventura.

I should be happy. Instead I feel empty.

"Why was it so important to us to get revenge?" I ask Amalita as we sit in side-by-side chairs getting our hair trimmed and blown out.

"Revenge feels good," she says, checking out her reflection in the salon mirror. "Someone hurts you, you hurt them back. It's biblical. Don't mess with the Bible."

"Does it make you feel good?" I ask. Because it isn't working that way for me.

"Are you kidding? Did you see Taylor moping around when Reenzie only wanted to hang on you? *Delicioso*."

"Right. I get that," I say, sighing. "But did it make you feel better about you guys not being friends anymore?"

Amalita meets my gaze in the mirror. "No. That will always and forever . . . suck."

I think about when Taylor followed me into the library, the way she said I didn't know the whole story, and how she seemed almost jealous of my friendship with Amalita. "You ever think maybe it sucks for her too?"

"*Eso es ridículo*," she says. "If she feels bad, she knows where to find me. I didn't change."

I see my mom's car when we come out of the salon. The plan is for her to swing by Amalita's place so Ames can get her clothes for tonight; then we'll go to my house to get ready.

"You know, would it be okay if we don't get ready together?" I ask Amalita as we get into the car. "My stomach is really bothering me."

I clearly need to sit down and make a list of better excuses. The stomach thing is getting old.

"No," Amalita says, blanching. "It's not okay."

"Please, I'm so sorry," I say, wincing. "I just want to lie down for a while. Do you think you could get a ride to my place and be there around six?"

"You're not serious."

"I think she is, Amalita," my mother says, turning to look at me. "She looks a little pale."

I *always* look a little pale, but I'll take whatever help I can get. Amalita isn't happy about the change, but she agrees only after I pinkie swear to do my makeup exactly as she's instructed. When I get home, Mom tells me to get some rest and promises to wake me in time to get ready for the Night of Dreams, but I have other plans.

There's someone I have to call, and an email I have to send.

▼

At 5:45, the doorbell rings. Amalita's outside in a shimmery black dress with shoes, earrings, and bracelets to match. By now I've told Mom and Erick the plan, so they say nothing as Amalita continues to ring the bell, then bang on the door. Then she calls my cell.

"Autumn!" she cries impatiently. "Open up! Don't tell me you're Reenzie-ing me! I will never forgive you if that's what you're doing, Autumn Falls!"

Through the peephole, I see another car pull up to the curb. Taylor steps out of the passenger side. She's dressed in a long silver sheath dress that makes her look even taller and leaner than she already is. The driver beeps a hello/good-bye, then pulls away.

Taylor looks confused as she starts up my walkway. "Amalita?"

"Taylor?" Now Amalita's the one who looks bewildered. "Um . . . what are you doing here?"

"I'm going with Autumn to the Night of Dreams with Kyler Leeds," she says slowly. "At least, I thought I was."

"Well, that's just great," Amalita says, glaring over at the door. "Because that's why I'm here."

And then the two former friends look at each other and simultaneously realize what's happening. Amalita wheels around and starts banging on the door.

"I'm gonna kill you, Autumn!"

"Oh, that'll make her want to come out," Taylor says sarcastically.

Amalita spins back. "Do you have a better idea?"

Taylor shrugs. She stands there, motionless for a minute, and then blurts out, "I've missed you, Ames."

Amalita freezes. I've never seen her so still. Slowly she turns and looks Taylor in the eye. "Seriously?"

Taylor blushes and looks at her feet. "Well . . . yeah. Of course."

"Of course?" Ames scoffs. "'Cause to me you've looked pretty happy with your new little *cuate* crew."

"Stop," Taylor says. "Don't be like that. I can have other friends and still be your friend too."

Ames raises an eyebrow and tries to stare her down, but this time Taylor looks her square in the eye and doesn't budge. I wonder if they're both too stubborn and my plan is doomed.

Then a smile plays at the corners of Amalita's lips. "So did you know Autumn was doing this?"

"No clue," Taylor admits.

"Pretty sneaky."

"Totally. I'd even say it's devious and presumptuous."

"Oooh, that's good," Ames agrees. She turns toward the door and shouts, "You hear that, Autumn? Devious and presumptuous!" Then she looks back to Taylor. "Gimme some more SAT words, Tee. What else have you got?"

"*Scelestic*," she suggests. "It means 'evil.'"

Amalita manages a small smile. "J.J. would kiss your feet if he heard that."

"Jack's more the foot guy."

I smile on my side of the door. Then Amalita screams and grabs Taylor's arm. I move from the peephole to the kitchen window and spot the limo pulling into the driveway. For a second I feel like an idiot. Kyler Leeds could be in that limo right now. Am I really going to stay in my kitchen?

A man—not Kyler Leeds—gets out the passenger-side door.

"Amalita and Taylor, I presume? I'm Donovan, Kyler

Leeds's assistant. Are you ready to begin your Night of Dreams?"

Taylor can't even speak. Amalita squeals as she forgets that she hates Taylor, clinging to her arm and jumping up and down.

Donovan opens the back door of the limo. I can't see anything inside. Taylor and Amalita exchange a look, grinning at each other in a way that wipes out any doubt about my choice, then race for the door. As they pile in I hear a pair of earsplitting shrieks. I watch the limo drive away until I can't see it anymore. Only then do I realize my phone is ringing. It's J.J.

"Hey," I say as I walk back up to my room with the phone to my ear.

"Got an interesting call from Taylor today," he says. "She wanted to know if she could trust you."

"You said absolutely not and that I'm an abomination to all that is trustworthy and good?"

"Something like that," he says, laughing.

"They're on their way to the Night of Dreams right now," I tell him.

"And you're on the phone with me. You clearly got the better end of the deal."

I laugh out loud. "Clearly."

"Interesting thing," J.J. says. "There's not a single anagram for *mensch*. If that's what you are, that's what you are, no matter how you look at it."

"Taylor used the word *scelestic*," I share.

"I need to play Scrabble immediately. Come over, I'll call Jack."

"Next time," I promise. "There's something I've got to do first."

Luckily, Mom is impressed enough by my act of generosity that she's willing to chauffeur. We drop Erick off at his new friend Anthony's house; then she drops me off and promises she'll come back whenever I text.

It's dark, but the house next to Reenzie's is well lit. I walk up the front path and ring the bell. After a moment I hear footsteps and take a deep breath to calm my pounding heart.

"Go home, Autumn." It's Sean.

Stupid peephole. I push myself close to the door. "Sean, wait! Please!"

I stay perfectly still, but I don't hear any more footsteps. He's still there.

"Just give me a minute, and then if you want to slam the door in my face it's okay."

Sean opens the door. Then he steps outside and pulls it shut behind him. He frowns. "You're wearing a Peyton Manning jersey."

"I am," I say. The jersey belongs to Erick and is actually a little small on me, but it can't be helped. "And this"— I nod to the thing I'm shifting from hand to hand— "is a football. At least, that's what they tell me."

No response. It's like talking to a Buckingham Palace guard.

"I was wondering if you wanted to maybe throw the ball around," I say, trying to stay nonchalant. "I hear you're pretty good. Star quarterback and all."

"Can't," he says. "Reenzie's here. She was pretty upset, thought she'd be doing something else tonight. So I had her over."

"Right. Sorry. Well, I'm not here to play football, obviously," I begin. "I just . . . I wanted you to know that I really like the way you said you saw me. It's who I want to be, and I don't know that I would have seen it without you, so . . . thanks."

I turn to walk away.

"Autumn, wait. I talked to Reenzie about the site," he calls after me.

I spin around.

"I didn't tell her what you found. I just pressed her on it. She didn't admit anything, but I know her well enough. . . . I believe what you said."

"Sorry," I say. I know it has to hurt him. He always defended her.

"We all make mistakes. Sometimes pretty bad ones."

He says it looking right into my eyes, and I'm not sure if he's talking about Reenzie's mistakes, mine, or his own.

"Bye, Sean."

"Maybe next weekend," he says when I'm halfway down his walk.

"What?"

"To throw the ball around. I'm around next weekend."

It's like the sun came out at night. I feel warm all over.

"You sure about that?" I ask. "'Cause I won't take it easy on you."

"I'd never want you to," he says. "See you, Autumn."

He closes the door and I smile as I text Mom to pick me up at the opening of the development. As I walk the blocks to meet her, my phone buzzes. Amalita has sent me a photo of her and Taylor, with Kyler Leeds wedged in between them. They all look ridiculously happy.

TONITE IS AWESOME! THANK YOU,
AUTUMN!!!!

And then I get another text.

Hey, Autumn, your friends told me what you did
for them, and I think you're absolutely brilliant.
Hope I can meet you one day and tell you in
person. XOXO Kyler

I press my phone to my heart as a little sunbeam of happiness shoots through me. At that exact moment I glance up and see someone familiar standing in the shadows on the lawn. It's a man, and even though it's dark, I can somehow tell that he's smiling at me.

A car comes by and the headlights blind me for a second. When I look back at the lawn, the man's gone, but I know who I saw. And what I felt.

"Hey, Dad," I whisper into the night. "Thanks for the Thing. I'll try to use it to make you proud. I love you."

I blow a kiss to the darkness, then keep on walking.

acknowledgments

Thank you to everyone who made *Autumn Falls* happen:

Thor Bradwell, my friend and manager, for always having my back and supporting me, and for all the funny jokes and secrets we share. Adam Griffin and Ryan Bundra, for always believing in me and for making this dream possible. Brian Barwick, for being the homie and keeping me organized: your job is never done. Laura Ackermann and Alex Heller, for always encouraging me, having snacks available, and making sure the world knows me the way I really am. Howard Fishman, for your negotiating skills and professional advice. Matthew Elblonk, for the constant reminders when something is due, for putting in motion a great book deal, and for being my support.

My Disney Channel Family and Hollywood Records, for pushing me to do my best and helping me discover and develop talents that I never knew I had. Without you guys, none of this would have been possible, at least not at this point. Chris Thompson, for being my dad figure. When others said NO, you said YES. Rob Lotterstein, for your snarky wit, which has rubbed off on me and come in handy many times.

Delacorte Press, for giving me this opportunity; I am ever so grateful. Wendy Loggia, Beverly Horowitz, and Dominique Cimina, for assisting me in making this the best book and experience I could ever have imagined, and for your impressive notes and pure excitement about the book. Elise Allen, my collaborator, my friend, for always being there, for having an incredible wealth of imagination and talent, and for making sure we've told a very warm and personal story. Maddie, you are adorable, and I enjoyed our breakfast together when you came with Elise and we started on this long journey. It's a memory I will always hold close to my heart.

Thanks also to Tristan Klier, my high school sweetheart, for your hours of tutoring and for being my best friend and the inspiration for the young romance in the series. To Kailey, Olivia, Bella P., and Claudia, for being great girls and the best of besties any girl could ask for. To Stephan Muskus, for making me ramen noodles when I have reading, writing, or any other type of work to do. To Remy, Dani, and Kaili for being the greatest friends and siblings I ever could have dreamed of; for being more than family: you are my heart. To Louis V and Kingston, my loving pets and companions, for reminding me not to work so hard by either stealing my homework or sitting on my computer and making me laugh. To my grandma and my dad, for being my guardian angels who are working in heaven to keep me safe and on the right path. I feel your presence any time I make a decision. You were both big inspirations in my book. To my mother, my best friend, my partner in crime, the peanut butter to my jelly, the one who holds our family together and inspires me every day to find the good in the world and make it even better.

Lastly, to all those with learning disabilities: I hope my journey inspires you to never give up on your dreams. You can achieve what you set your mind to. As my dad—and possibly Calvin Coolidge—used to say, "Persistence breaks resistance."